AN
INSIGNIFICANT
CASE

AN INSIGNIFICANT CASE

A THRILLER

PHILLIP MARGOLIN

MINOTAUR
BOOKS
NEW YORK

First published in the United States by Minotaur Books,
an imprint of St. Martin's Publishing Group

AN INSIGNIFICANT CASE. Copyright © 2024 by Phillip Margolin. All rights reserved. Printed in the United States of America. For information, address St. Martin's Publishing Group, 120 Broadway, New York, NY 10271.

www.minotaurbooks.com

Designed by Omar Chapa

Library of Congress Cataloging-in-Publication Data

Names: Margolin, Phillip, author.
Title: An insignificant case : a thriller / Phillip Margolin.
Description: First edition. | New York : Minotaur Books, 2024.
Identifiers: LCCN 2024022626 | ISBN 9781250885821 (hardcover) |
    ISBN 9781250885838 (ebook)
Subjects: LCGFT: Thrillers (Fiction) | Novels.
Classification: LCC PS3563.A649 I57 2024 | DDC 813/.54—dc23/
    eng/20240517
LC record available at https://lccn.loc.gov/2024022626

Our books may be purchased in bulk for promotional, educational, or business use. Please contact your local bookseller or the Macmillan Corporate and Premium Sales Department at 1-800-221-7945, extension 5442, or by email at MacmillanSpecialMarkets@macmillan.com.

First Edition: 2024

10 9 8 7 6 5 4 3 2 1

For Judy Margolin, who has earned her nickname
"Saint Judy." Fingers crossed.

PART ONE
THE MARTYR

CHAPTER ONE

GUIDO SABATINI WALKED INTO LA BELLA ROMA ITALIAN RISTORANTE A few moments before Gretchen Hall left her office to tell her maître d' that she had resolved a problem with one of their suppliers. Guido looked like some of the religious paintings of Jesus that Gretchen had seen in cathedrals and churches. He was six foot four and dressed in a white floor-length caftan that was secured at the waist by a gold rope. His thick blond hair flowed over his shoulders, and his downy beard and mustache framed a beatific smile that beamed at Salvatore Borelli while the maître d' berated him.

Gretchen, the owner of La Bella Roma, was on the downside of forty, but she could have passed for someone much younger. Her hair was as blond as the biblical figure who was standing in front of her maître d', and her black pantsuit and white, man-tailored silk blouse clung to a figure that a teenage girl would have envied.

"What's the problem, Sal?" Gretchen asked.

Borelli turned toward his boss. "This guy came in last week.

He's trying to hawk his pictures to our customers. I told him to get lost then, and I'm telling him again. If he's not outta here in two seconds, I'm calling the cops."

It was the height of the lunch hour, and a restless crowd was stacking up behind the artist. Gretchen saw that the object of Borelli's ire was holding a portfolio. To avoid a scene, Gretchen opted for diplomacy.

"What kind of pictures do you have for sale?" Gretchen asked.

"Not pictures, signora, works of art," the man said in a poor imitation of an Italian accent. "Paintings of martyred saints, landscapes of Tuscan hill towns, depictions of the canals of Venice."

"Why don't we go to my office so I can take a look?"

Gretchen turned, and the artist followed her to the back of the restaurant between tables of gawking diners.

Gretchen's office was starkly modern and windowless. She had decorated it with a granite-topped desk, a black leather sofa, and black-and-white photographs of the Colosseum, the Via Veneto, the Piazza Navona, and other landmarks of the Eternal City. The only anomaly was a mirror with an ornate gold frame that had belonged to a mistress of one of the doges. Hall had found it in an antique store in Milan during Fashion Week and had fallen in love with the story of its origin. The mirror was mounted on the wall across from a photograph of the Trevi Fountain.

"I'm Gretchen Hall, and I own La Bella Roma," she said when they were inside her office. "Who might you be?"

"I am Guido Sabatini, signora."

A small glass-topped coffee table covered with menus, invoices, and other papers stood under the photograph of the fountain. Gretchen cleared the tabletop.

"Well, Guido, let's see what you've got."

Sabatini opened his portfolio, and Gretchen was stunned. The artist had created the optical illusion of a Saint Sebastian who writhed in pain from the arrows that pierced him. The crowds wandering the street of a Tuscan hill town actually seemed to move. But it was a moonlit view of a Venice canal that Gretchen decided she had to have.

"They're not bad," said Gretchen, who had been taught how to bargain at an early age by her attorney father. "What do you want for the Venice canal painting?"

"One thousand dollars, signora," Guido said.

"Oh, well. I really like it, but one thousand dollars . . ." She shrugged. "I could manage two hundred and fifty."

Guido knew what Gretchen was doing, and he didn't really care about money. His art was his passion, and seeing it displayed where others could be awed by it was what really motivated him.

"For you, signora, I will make a sacrifice. You can have my painting for five hundred dollars."

Five hundred dollars was nothing to Gretchen, and Guido looked like he could use the money.

"Done," she said as she moved the painting to her desk. "I don't suppose you take credit cards?"

Guido smiled. "Cash only, signora."

Gretchen returned the smile. "Of course."

While Guido gathered up his other paintings and returned them to his portfolio, Gretchen took down the photo of the Trevi Fountain, revealing a wall safe. She punched in the combination on the keypad, opened the safe, and reached inside. When her hand came out, it was wrapped around a wad of bills. Gretchen counted out five hundred dollars, put the rest back in the safe, closed it, and hung the photo back on the wall.

"Do me a favor, Guido," Gretchen said as she held out the money. "Don't come back to La Bella Roma. I appreciate your talent, but Sal has a hard-on for you, and a scene is not good for business."

"No problem," Guido promised as he pushed the money into a pocket in the caftan.

"I'm glad you came in. I really like the painting."

Guido bowed and left. As soon as the door closed behind him, Gretchen held up the painting in front of the wall safe. She liked the photo of the fountain, but she loved the scene from one of her favorite places.

GUIDO DROVE INTO THE YARD IN FRONT OF HIS FARMHOUSE AND WENT up to his bedroom. He opened the top drawer in his chest of drawers and took out a metal box where he kept his money. Five hundred was a good sale, but he hadn't sold enough paintings to pay his expenses for the month. That meant he would have to become Lawrence Weiss tonight, something he only did when there was an emergency.

As soon as the sun went down, Guido traded his caftan for faded jeans, a plaid shirt, and a Seattle Mariners baseball cap. Then he drove to a store that sold guns in a strip mall in Clackamas County.

Guido walked over to the cashier and gave him the password. The cashier nodded toward a door at the back of the store. A large man with a day-old beard and a bouncer's build opened the door, and Guido repeated the password. The man stepped aside and let Guido into a back room where men and a few women sat around three tables playing poker.

Guido had played against a few of them after the casinos had blackballed him and forced him out of the high-stakes games. They would be easy pickings, but he had to be careful about how much money he won, because some of the players were sore losers and could be violent.

Guido took a seat at one of the tables and played modestly while he sized up the opposition. There was one old-timer who played a decent game, two players who had no idea what they were doing but thought they did, and Brad and Brent Atkins, two brothers who had tells that flashed like a neon sign whenever they were bluffing. The brothers looked like hard cases, so Guido only took advantage of them a few times, but the pots he won from them were the biggest of the night.

Guido acted like he wasn't sure he would win those pots and apologized to the loser as if he were embarrassed by his luck, but one of the brothers didn't look like he was buying the aw-shucks routine.

When Guido had cleared $3,000, he decided it was time to quit. There was another game in Washington County he could hit tomorrow that had slightly higher stakes.

"Night, boys," Guido said. "Thanks for letting me play in your game."

Guido heard two chairs scraping against the floor just before he left the back room. When he was outside and hidden in the shadows at the side of the building, he focused on the door to the gun store. Seconds later, the brothers walked into the parking lot.

"I have a gun and I will shoot you," Guido said.

The brothers whirled toward the sound of Guido's voice, but they couldn't see Guido until he stepped out of the shadows with his gun trained on them.

"You play poker as poorly as you play the role of robbers. Please go back to the game and don't come out for twenty minutes."

Brad hesitated, but Brent moved his hand toward his coat.

"I can see you going for the poorly concealed gun you're hiding under your coat. Please stop and go inside."

"You ain't gonna shoot us," Brent said.

Guido pointed his pistol at Brent's heart.

"You have a tell that let me know every time you were bluffing. That's how I won those hands from you. Were you able to tell when I was bluffing? If you can, go for your gun. If you can't, go inside so I don't have to shoot you."

Brad touched his sibling's shoulder. "Let's go, Brent. It ain't worth it."

Brent glared at Guido. "You better not show your face here again," he threatened before following his brother inside.

Moments later, Guido drove away from the strip mall and headed home.

CHAPTER TWO

IF CHARLIE WEBB WERE A GRADE, HE WOULD HAVE BEEN A C, WHICH was the average grade he received starting in elementary school and ending in law school. Charlie had average looks too—brown hair, brown eyes, a pleasant smile, and a nice but not awe-inspiring build.

Charlie never raised his hand in class, and his teachers rarely called on him. He wasn't in any extracurricular activities, except football. He was always big for his age, so his high school coach put him on the offensive line. Charlie was a serviceable guard without the talent it took to get a college scholarship, so he started at a community college, then got his four-year degree at Portland State University, where he graduated—surprise—in the middle of his class.

Charlie watched a lot of lawyer shows on TV, so he applied to law school. He was self-aware enough to forget Harvard, Yale, and any other school in the top fifty, but it was discouraging to be rejected by every second-tier school to which he applied. Then, just when it looked like he was going to have to figure out another way to earn a living, he was accepted at Oxford School of Law, a third-tier law school that had no connection to *the* Oxford University and gave its students loans at suspiciously high interest rates. Three years later, Charlie passed the bar and was forced to hang out a shingle when nobody offered him a job.

Charlie's law practice limped along on court appointments, divorce clients referred by family members, and referrals from two of his fellow high school linemen, who were members of the Barbarians motorcycle club. The Barbarians were always running afoul of the law and supplied his only steady customers.

On Monday morning, Charlie was assigned to the courtroom of the Honorable Iris Carter, who was going to hear the case of *State of Oregon v. Peter Easley.*

Peter Easley's gift was the ability to blend in. His height and weight were average. His hair was a dull brown shade, and he had no tattoos, scars, or other features that would attract anyone's attention.

Easley's nickname among the Barbarians was "the Ghost" because of his supernatural ability to move illegal drugs without being detected. Unfortunately, Easley had run into some Ghostbusters during a traffic stop, and a packet of cocaine had been found in a secret pocket in the headrest on the driver's side of his dull brown Toyota.

Charlie had filed a pretrial motion to suppress the evidence on the grounds that the cocaine had been found during an illegal and unconstitutional warrantless search of Peter's car that had been conducted without probable cause. His motion had been met with disdain and derision by Bridget Fournier, the Multnomah County deputy district attorney who had been assigned Easley's case.

Charlie hadn't slept very well the night before the hearing. This was the biggest criminal case he'd handled for the Barbarians or any other client, and Bridget Fournier had a terrifying reputation. Charlie had asked some of his friends in the criminal defense bar about her, and they all gave their condolences. The consensus was that Fournier was very, very smart, had no sense of humor, and gave no quarter.

Many of the members of the Barbarians were waiting for Charlie and his client in the corridor outside Judge Carter's courtroom. They wore their colors, sported beards and tattoos, and would have seemed very scary to the average citizen. Charlie was on friendly terms with many members of the gang, but he was always on his toes around them because he was well aware of their capacity for violence.

Bob Malone and Gary Schwartz had played on the offensive line with Charlie in high school. They clapped him on the back and gave Charlie a thumbs-up. Then they yelled, "Go, Stallions!" the nickname of their high school football team, before following Charlie and Easley into the courtroom, where they found seats on the spectator benches with other members of the club.

Charlie said hello to Bridget Fournier when he walked through the bar of the court on the way to his seat at the defense counsel table. She returned the greeting with a terse reply before turning her eyes back to the memo she had written in opposition to Charlie's motion.

Fournier, who was in her early thirties, used the bare minimum of makeup and wore no jewelry. She had pale blue eyes, a straight nose, thin lips, and a full figure that would have been sexy in the fifties when movie stars like Marilyn Monroe carried a few extra pounds. Fournier's courtroom ensemble consisted of a white blouse and a gray pantsuit. Her straight black hair fell just below the shoulders of her suit jacket. Charlie didn't think Fournier was pretty, but she wasn't plain. He did think that a touch of makeup, a brighter outfit, and some nice jewelry might have tipped the balance to the pretty side.

Easley's case had been assigned to Iris Carter, a slender African American in her early fifties who had been appointed to the Multnomah County Circuit Court ten years earlier after a successful career in private practice.

"The State calls Portland police officer Garrett Strom," Fournier said as soon as Judge Carter took the bench.

Charlie had made a motion to have the witnesses, who were all police officers, wait outside the courtroom so they couldn't hear one another's testimony. He'd made an exception for Strom, who was the first witness.

Strom was a shade over six feet with a compact build, a buzz cut, and dark brown eyes.

"Officer Strom, how long have you been on the force?" Fournier asked.

"Ten years."

"On the evening of December tenth of last year, were you on patrol in Southeast Portland?"

"I was."

"Did you come in contact with the defendant, Peter Easley?"

"I did."

"Did you know Mr. Easley?"

"Only by his reputation as a drug dealer. Before that evening, I'd never met him."

Judge Carter looked at Charlie, waiting for him to object to Strom's characterization of his client, but Charlie stayed silent.

"Please tell Judge Carter about your interaction with the defendant on the evening of December 10."

The officer turned toward the judge. "Mr. Easley's Toyota was parked outside the Bald Eagle Tavern between two other cars. I was on patrol in the area with Dennis Newsome, a recent academy graduate, when I saw the defendant get in his vehicle and start it. Then he backed into the car behind him with enough force to dent the bumper. He pulled forward and rammed into the car in front of him. Then he managed to get out of the space and drive away.

"I put on my lights and siren and followed him two blocks before he pulled over and jumped out of his car. I had broadcast the defendant's name and the make of his car when I followed him, because I wasn't sure if he would pull over.

"Mr. Easley was belligerent, and I suspected that he had been drinking. He swore at me and asked me in a very loud voice why I had stopped him. I told him that he had hit two cars and driven away without leaving insurance information. He denied damaging the cars and began screaming about police harassment. I became concerned about his behavior. I was also nervous because a crowd was starting to form."

"Did any other officers arrive on the scene?"

"Yes. Sergeant Malcom Broadstreet drove up with Anthony Townes, a rookie he was training."

"What happened then?" Fournier asked.

"Sergeant Broadstreet asked me why I had stopped the defendant, and I told him what I'd seen. The sergeant appeared to know the defendant, and they got into a verbal confrontation. The crowd was getting unruly, and I was occupied with keeping order. At some point, Sergeant Broadstreet handcuffed the defendant and put him in the back of his patrol car."

"Did he give you any instructions concerning Mr. Easley's car?"

"Yes. He told me to have officers Townes and Newsome conduct an inventory search of Mr. Easley's car, then have it towed to the impound lot."

"What is an inventory search?"

"When we impound a car, we go through it to record the contents so we have a list of valuables and other things that are in the car in case there is a problem later on with the owner claiming that something is missing."

"Do you need a search warrant or probable cause to conduct an inventory search?"

"No, ma'am."

Charlie had researched inventory searches after reading Fournier's memo, and he knew this was true. He also knew that he would lose his motion if the plan he'd formulated failed.

"What happened during the inventory search?"

"Officer Townes discovered cocaine in the headrest on the driver's side of the car."

"I have no further questions, Your Honor," Fournier said.

"Mr. Webb," Judge Carter said.

"Didn't Officer Townes find the cocaine in a secret compartment in the Toyota's headrest?"

"Yes."

"Did Sergeant Broadstreet ask officers Townes and Newsome to search for drugs?"

"No."

"Searching the car for drugs would have been illegal, wouldn't it, because you did not have a warrant or probable cause to believe that drugs were in the car?"

"That's correct."

"So, the discovery of the cocaine was fortuitous?"

"Yes."

"No further questions."

"The State calls Sergeant Broadstreet."

Malcom Broadstreet's short black hair was streaked with gray, but the rest of his stocky body looked like it was defeating the aging process. He had the broad chest and thick arms of someone who pumped iron and the confident stride of someone who was used to being in charge.

"Sergeant Broadstreet, how long have you been a Portland police officer?" the deputy district attorney asked.

"Twenty years come October."

"On the evening of December tenth, did you come in contact with the defendant?"

"I did."

"Tell the judge what happened."

Broadstreet smiled at the judge. "Good morning, Your Honor," Broadstreet said in a way that let Charlie know that this was not the first time he'd been in Judge Carter's court. "On the evening of December tenth, I was training Tony Townes, a new recruit, when I heard Officer Strom on my radio say that he was having a problem with Peter Easley. I drove over to help out and found Easley yelling at Officer Strom and acting in a very aggressive way. I intervened and eventually arrested the defendant. After I placed him in the back of my vehicle, I told Townes and Dennis Newsome, who was also new to the force, to make an inventory search of Mr. Easley's car before having it towed to the impound lot. While they were inventorying the car, Officer Townes found cocaine concealed in the headrest on the driver's side."

"No further questions."

"Sergeant Broadstreet," Charlie said, "this isn't the first time you've arrested Mr. Easley, is it?"

"No."

"In fact, you've arrested him six times, haven't you?"

"That sounds right."

"Did any of these arrests result in a conviction?"

Broadstreet's cheeks flushed. "No."

"Isn't it true that you've told people on several occasions that you won't be able to have a good night's sleep until you've put Mr. Easley behind bars?"

"I may have said something like that."

"Did you have a conversation with Mr. Easley in the street before you arrested him?"

"Yes."

"Did you accuse him of selling dope to little children?"

"I may have."

"Did he say that he sold dope to your mother?"

"Yes," Broadstreet answered as the red color of his cheeks darkened.

"You don't like my client, do you?"

"That's obvious."

"You hate him, don't you?"

"I think he's scum. Does that answer your question?"

Charlie smiled. "Thank you for your honesty, Sergeant Broadstreet. Were you surprised when Officer Townes found cocaine in Mr. Easley's car?"

"No."

"You suspected he might have a controlled substance secreted somewhere in the Toyota, didn't you?"

"Knowing Peter, I thought it was possible."

"No further questions."

"The State rests," Fournier said.

"I'd like to question Officer Townes," Charlie said.

Anthony Townes looked like he'd just graduated from junior high school. The slender rookie had wavy blond hair and fair skin, and he fidgeted in the witness-box.

Charlie smiled. "Hi, Officer Townes. You look a little nervous. Is this your first time testifying under oath in court?"

"Yes."

"I'll give you the advice I give everyone I call as a witness. Just tell the truth and you'll do just fine. So, I understand you just graduated from the police academy."

Townes nodded.

"Officer Townes," the judge said. "You have to answer out loud for the record."

Townes blushed. "Sorry. Yes. I just graduated."

"Congratulations. You're fortunate to have Sergeant Broadstreet as a mentor. He's a very experienced officer. Was the incident with my client the first time you were involved in an arrest?"

"No. There was one other time a few days before."

"What about conducting a search? Had you done that before?"

"No, this was my first time."

"What was the sergeant's reaction when he heard that Peter Easley was creating a disturbance?"

"He, uh, he got excited."

"I assume he explained that my client was a notorious drug dealer?"

"Yeah, he did."

"Someone he was dying to take off the streets because of all the harm he caused?"

"Yes, sir."

"Given Mr. Easley's criminal history as someone who deals drugs, I assume that the sergeant was certain he'd have drugs on his person or in his vehicle."

"He said that Mr. Easley never left home without narcotics," he answered with a smile.

Charlie stared for a moment. Then he laughed. "I get it. That's like the American Express commercial. 'Don't leave home without it,' right?"

Townes blushed and grinned. "That's the one."

"Now, I've been to the impound lot and looked inside Mr. Easley's car. That hidden pocket in the headrest is really hard to see."

Townes nodded. "Sergeant Broadstreet said the defendant wouldn't hide his narcotics in any place that was obvious."

Bridget Fournier had barely paid any attention to Charlie's direct examination, but now she stiffened.

"Didn't it make sense that Sergeant Broadstreet would tell you to look for drugs in a hidden compartment in the Toyota since he knew how clever Mr. Easley is?"

"Yes, sir. The sergeant said we probably wouldn't find the defendant's stash unless we were really disciplined."

Charlie noticed that Bridget Fournier was paler than usual.

"How long did it take for you to find the cocaine?"

"It wasn't easy. I'd almost given up when Dennis—that's Officer Newsome—told me to check around the headrest."

Charlie smiled. "No further questions."

Judge Carter turned to Townes. "Do I understand that Sergeant Broadstreet asked you to search Mr. Easley's Toyota for drugs?" she asked.

"Yes, ma'am," Townes answered.

"Do you have any questions of this witness, Miss Fournier?" the judge asked.

"No," Fournier answered. She looked furious.

"Do you have any more witnesses, Mr. Webb?" the judge asked.

"No, Your Honor."

"Thank you, Officer Townes. You're dismissed.

"Do you have anything to say?" Judge Carter asked Bridget as soon as the door closed behind Townes.

Fournier looked like she was going to throw up.

"I . . . No. This is embarrassing."

"I'll say," the judge told Fournier. "I'm going to grant Mr. Webb's motion, and I suggest that you have a heart-to-heart with Sergeant Broadstreet and Officer Strom. Thank goodness we had the testimony of a naive rookie who hasn't learned how to cover up illegal conduct yet. Court's adjourned."

Easley leaped up and hugged Charlie. "That was fucking awesome."

Charlie looked over Easley's shoulder and saw his opponent fight her way through the Barbarians, who were surging toward the front of the courtroom. Charlie actually felt a little sorry for Fournier. He assumed that Broadstreet and Strom had lied to her. He didn't feel the least bit sorry for the two policemen, but he hoped that Townes didn't get in any trouble.

"Drinks are on me!" Easley shouted as the crowd dragged Charlie toward the courtroom door. Noon was several hours away, but Charlie knew that the Barbarians would not see that as an excuse for staying sober. So, he accepted the praise and went along with the crowd that was headed for the Buccaneer Tavern.

CHAPTER THREE

THE JUSTICE CENTER WAS A SIXTEEN-STORY BUILDING IN DOWNTOWN Portland that housed the Multnomah County jail, several courtrooms, and the Portland Police Central Precinct among other things. The detective division of the Central Precinct was a wide-open space that stretched along one side of the thirteenth floor. Each detective had his or her own cubicle that was separated from the other detectives' by a chest-high divider.

Yesterday evening, Detective Sally Blaisedale had been part of a team that had raided a house where a cartel was storing narcotics and cash. The raid had resulted in several arrests, and it was early morning before the prisoners had been interrogated and processed. Most of the participants in the raid had gone home to snatch a few hours of sleep, but Sally had stayed at the Justice Center to write her reports.

Blaisedale's intercom buzzed after she'd been working on the reports for an hour.

"There's a woman on the line who wants to talk to a detective. Do you want to take the call?" the receptionist asked.

Blaisedale needed a break, so she told the receptionist to put the call through.

"How can I help you?" Blaisedale asked.

"Are you a detective?" the woman asked. Sally thought she sounded young and frightened.

"Yes."

"We want to talk to you about something terrible that happened to us."

"There's more than one of you?"

"There were a lot of girls, but it's just us two who want to meet with you."

"Okay. Do you want to come to my office at police headquarters?"

"No. We can't risk going to police headquarters. They might be watching us."

"Who might be watching?"

"We'll tell you when we meet. Can you go to the Thai restaurant in Hillsdale in the mall across from Ida B. Wells High School?"

"Are you a student?"

"Please. Can you meet us?"

"Okay. When?"

"After school. Three thirty."

DETECTIVE BLAISEDALE WAS SEATED IN A BOOTH AT THE BACK OF THE restaurant, dressed in jeans, a Trailblazers sweatshirt, and a Blazers ball cap while she read a mystery novel and sipped a Thai iced coffee. When the girls came in, she had no trouble spotting them. They were the only women of high school age in the restaurant who weren't smiling and who looked scared.

Blaisedale made eye contact, and the girls hurried to the booth. They were both wearing jeans and hoodies. When they sat down, the hoodies fell back.

"Hi," Blaisedale said as she flashed a smile that she hoped assured them that they were safe. "I'm Sally Blaisedale. I'm a detective. Who are you?"

"I'm Kendra Miles, and this is Felicity Halston."

Miles was five three with curly black hair, high cheekbones, and blue eyes. Halston was two inches taller than her friend and had long, straight blond hair and a pug nose.

"Nice to meet you," Blaisedale said. "Now, how can I help you?"

"Before we tell you," Kendra Miles said, "we need to know that you'll protect us."

"I'll need to know what this is about before I can work out the best way to do that."

"What if this involves very powerful people with a lot of political influence?"

The detective looked directly at the girls. "No one is above the law. If you have evidence that a powerful person committed a crime, I'll go after him the same way I'd go after anyone else."

The girls looked at each other. Blaisedale thought that they were really scared, but they also looked determined.

"We were kidnapped, taken to an estate in the country, and forced to have sex."

Miles stopped and took a deep breath. Halston wrapped an arm around her shoulders and hugged her.

"I can see that this is very hard for you," Blaisedale said. "Take your time."

"I want you to know what they did to us," Miles said as a tear ran down her cheek.

CHAPTER FOUR

TWO WEEKS AFTER GRETCHEN HALL BOUGHT HIS PAINTING OF THE VEN-
ice canal, Guido Sabatini experienced an uncontrollable urge to
visit the dining room of La Bella Roma Italian Ristorante so
he could see the enraptured faces of the patrons as they gazed
upon one of his masterpieces. Guido knew that he had promised
Gretchen that he would not return to La Bella Roma. Unfortunately, impulse control was not an item that Guido stored in his
psychic toolbox.

When Guido made his entrance at the height of the lunch
hour, Salvatore Borelli's face turned an irate shade of red. Guido
scanned the dining room in search of a gondola passing under
a low stone bridge that crossed a narrow canal. The maître d'
smiled at the couple who were waiting to be seated and excused
himself.

"What are you doing here?" Borelli demanded.

"I have not returned to disturb your customers," Guido assured the maître d'. "I have missed my painting of Venezia, and I wanted to see her once more."

"Well, you won't see it in the dining room. Miss Hall hung it in her office, and you're not going in there."

Guido stared at Borelli in shock. "Signora Hall is hiding my masterpiece in her office, where no one can see it?"

"Didn't I just say that?"

"She can't do that."

"She owns the painting, so she can do what she wants with it. Now, why don't you take off so I can deal with people who want to have lunch?"

"Where is Signora Hall? I must speak to her about this. We must resolve this problem."

"Miss Hall isn't here, and she won't be here in the near future. She's out of state, and I don't know when she's going to return. So, unless you want lunch, get lost."

Guido drew himself up to his full height. "Signora Hall has insulted my painting by hiding it from your patrons. I will not rest until the insult has been avenged."

"Yeah, well, good luck with that. Now, are you going to leave, or do I have to call 911?"

Guido glared at Borelli. Then he turned on his heel and stomped out.

LA BELLA ROMA WAS AT ONE END OF A STRIP MALL THAT WAS PATROLLED by an elderly security guard, who made his rounds in a circle at the same time, on the same route, every hour. Guido Sabatini knew this, because he had staked out La Bella Roma for two nights after it closed. On the third night, as soon as the security guard was far enough from the restaurant, Guido walked to the rear door and used lock-picking skills he had learned from a thief he had met during his time consorting with shadowy characters in backroom poker games.

The restaurant had a primitive alarm system, and Guido disabled it quickly. Then he walked into Gretchen Hall's office. He used his flashlight to find his precious painting of the Venice canal. When he lifted it off the wall, he saw that Hall was using it to cover her wall safe. That made him furious. The painting was a work of art, not a decoration like a cheap, plastic wall sconce.

Guido had an amazing memory and an incredible facility with numbers, which helped him count cards, among other things. When Hall had opened the safe, Guido had seen the combination reflected in the ornate mirror that faced it. The numbers were backward in the mirror, but that was not a problem for Guido, who'd memorized the combination as easily as if he were reading it off a piece of paper.

Guido wanted revenge, and he hoped that there was something in the safe that he could use to blackmail Hall into hanging his masterpiece in the dining room, where all the restaurant's patrons would be able to see and appreciate it.

Guido played the beam of the flashlight around the safe's interior. Guido was not a thief, so he had no interest in the stacks of currency, and many of the papers he saw were too bulky to carry when he was also carrying his painting.

Guido was about to give up when the beam alighted on a small object. Why would Gretchen Hall be hiding it in her safe, he asked himself, and concluded that it must be important. Guido scooped up the flash drive and put it in his pocket. Then he left La Bella Roma and carried his booty to his car.

CHAPTER FIVE

AT NINE IN THE MORNING THE DAY AFTER GUIDO SABATINI BURGLARIZED La Bella Roma, Salvatore Borelli was standing in the open door of the restaurant, watching a police car park. A stocky, middle-aged police officer got out of the driver's side, and a muscular young policewoman got out of the passenger side. Borelli went to the sidewalk to greet them.

"Thanks for coming so fast. I'm Sal Borelli. I manage La Bella Roma."

"I'm Ken Jackman, and this is Sandy Tanaka," the male officer said. "What's the problem?"

"Someone broke in last night," Borelli said as he led the officers inside the restaurant. "The thief took a painting from my boss's office, and I know who he is. The security cameras took a beautiful picture of the son of a bitch."

"A painting?" Officer Jackman asked.

"Yeah. It was hanging over the safe. The bastard broke into that too."

"Was this an oil painting of a scene from Italy?" Jackman asked.

Borelli stopped in front of the door to Gretchen's office. "How did you know?"

"The thief isn't by any chance Guido Sabatini?"

Borelli stared at the officer. "What are you, Sherlock fucking Holmes?"

"I wish." Jackman sighed. "If I were that smart, I'd be a detective by now."

"Then how . . . ?"

"This isn't the first time Sabatini has pulled a stunt like this." Jackman looked at his partner.

"I make this the third," Tanaka said. "There was Bellini's and that steak house on Alder."

"What did he take this time?" Jackman asked.

"It's a painting of a gondola on a canal in Venice," Borelli answered.

"Show us the scene of the crime," Jackman said.

Borelli ushered the officers into Gretchen's office. The wall safe was open, but nothing else in the room appeared to have been disturbed.

"Do you know if Sabatini took anything from the safe?" Jackman asked.

"I don't know everything that was in it, but he left a lot of cash and some papers. You'll have to ask Miss Hall if there's anything missing."

"Miss Hall is . . . ?" Tanaka asked.

"Gretchen Hall. She owns the place."

"Is she coming in today?" Tanaka asked.

"No," Borelli said. "Hall's wealthy, and La Bella Roma is a hobby of hers. She'll come in a few times a month when she's in town, but I run the place most of the time. Miss Hall is in LA now with Leon Golden, the movie producer. He's got a picture nominated for an Oscar, and they're going to the Academy Awards."

"Do you know when she'll be back?"

"No, but I'll ask when I tell her about the robbery."

"Do that. She'll need to tell us if Sabatini took anything besides the painting. Meanwhile," Jackman said with a sigh, "we'll visit Guido and see if we can convince him to give back his ill-gotten gains."

The officers left. Borelli took out his phone to call his boss, but he stopped mid-dial. Gretchen would be having a great time in LA, and the painting was no big deal. Maybe the cops could get it back and he wouldn't have to upset her. Borelli decided to wait to tell Hall about the theft until she got back to Portland.

OFFICERS TANAKA AND JACKMAN CRUISED ALONG THE TWO-LANE country road that led to Guido Sabatini's farm. Overhead, white puff clouds floated across a clear blue sky and cast moving shadows over crops divided into earth-brown, sunflower-yellow, and emerald-green squares. The farmland rose up into hills thick with maples, oaks, and evergreens, and the officers were able to enjoy the pastoral scene, knowing that they would be confronting a harmless nutcase and not an armed, meth-crazed maniac.

The other time Jackman and Tanaka had come to the farm, they had recovered a painting that Guido had "liberated" from Bellini's restaurant. Sabatini had told them that he had purchased the farm a year earlier. When Jackman had asked him what he'd been doing before that, Guido had smiled and changed the subject. One thing was clear—Sabatini hadn't done much upkeep. The fields had gone to seed, and the exterior of the farmhouse and the red barn that Sabatini had turned into a studio looked the worse for wear.

Jackman parked the patrol car in the yard, and the officers walked into the barn. Painting supplies were spread across neatly stacked bales of hay that were within arm's reach of the artist's easel, where Sabatini was placing another arrow in Saint Sebastian's torso.

"Hey, Guido," Jackman said.

Sabatini paused his paintbrush halfway to his canvas.

"Officers Jackman and Tanaka! Welcome. To what do I owe the pleasure of this visit?"

"Don't be coy, Guido. You know why we're here," Jackman said.

"Honestly, I have no idea," Guido answered with a serene smile.

Jackman sighed. "Does the name *La Bella Roma Italian Ristorante* ring any bells?"

"I've never dined in the establishment, but I've heard wonderful things about their food."

"Come on, Guido," Tanaka said. "Don't make this like pulling teeth. You're the star of a movie recorded on the restaurant's security cameras."

"Give us the Venice canal painting and anything you took from the safe and we won't arrest you," Jackman said.

Sabatini's features darkened. "Gretchen Hall insulted me and my art. She does not deserve to look at my masterpiece."

"Yeah, well, she may not deserve to look at your painting, but she owns it," Jackman said. "We've explained this to you before. You're a bright guy, Guido, so you can't get away with saying that you don't understand that a person who pays you money for a painting owns it and can hang it where they want to."

"And hanging the painting in her office, where Miss Hall can see it all the time, isn't an insult," Tanaka said. "She wouldn't be able to see it as much if it was in the dining room, so that shows you she really likes your artwork."

"I do not honor an egotist who keeps my work where only she can see it and hides my masterpiece from a public that hungers for great art."

"Guido, if you're in jail, you can't paint," Tanaka said. "By refusing to give back one piece of art, you'll be depriving the world of more masterpieces."

"If you put me in jail, it is you who will be depriving the world of the works of Guido Sabatini."

Jackman sighed. "Are you gonna give us the painting? If you don't, we have to take you in, and the charge will be burglary, because you broke into the restaurant. That's a felony. It carries prison time. I like you, Guido. I think you're a hell of a painter, and I don't want to see you rot away in the Oregon State Pen. Please give us the painting."

Guido put down his paintbrush and held out his hands.

"Put on your handcuffs. I would rather be a martyr like Saint Sebastian than betray my art."

CHAPTER SIX

ON THE NIGHT BEFORE THE ACADEMY AWARDS, CHARLIE WEBB HAD many more than one too many at the Buccaneer Tavern, the hangout favored by his friends in the Barbarians motorcycle club.

Barbarians Bob Malone and Gary Schwartz drove the partially comatose attorney to his apartment house, a four-story brick building just off Northwest Nineteenth Avenue. Charlie's apartment was on the third floor, and the building did not have an elevator. Fortunately, Bob and Gary were huge, and they got Charlie up the stairs and tucked into bed without much trouble.

Charlie's apartment was very small. When he came home from work, he entered a short, narrow hall where a clothing rack and four large Tupperware containers filled with underwear, shirts, and other garments passed for a clothes closet. At the end of the hall was a bathroom that was just big enough for a narrow stall shower, a toilet, and a sink. Next to the bathroom was an L-shaped area. The section to the right of the bathroom was occupied by a sofa that sat across from a low table on which Charlie's television balanced. This area doubled as a bedroom when Charlie opened his sofa bed.

The apartment's only window did not add much light to the other section of the L. It looked out on the back wall of the apartment house next door and was covered with grime. A microwave sat on top of a small, squat refrigerator directly below the window and kitty-corner from a tiny sink. Charlie dined at a yellow Formica-topped table that stood in the shallow area in front of the sink.

Charlie fantasized that someday he would make enough money to buy a grand condo where he could hold wild parties, though who would attend these gatherings was a mystery, since his only close friends were left over from high school and Charlie had no steady girlfriend.

Charlie liked girls, and he was able to get dates since he was nice-looking and solid, but he was also boring, and the relationships didn't last. Sadly, more than one girl had broken his heart, because he always fell head over heels for someone who showed him any degree of affection.

When Charlie slipped out of sleep and into the real world on Sunday morning, his eyelids rose in slow motion and he struggled to focus. He managed to tilt his head so he could see the bright red digital readout on the clock on his nightstand. It was 10:05.

After staring at the ceiling for several minutes, Charlie sat up and was rewarded for his effort by the gift of a very painful bolt of lightning that ricocheted through the inside of his skull. He waited for the pain to subside. Then he staggered into the bathroom and let an ice-cold shower shock him awake. After he dressed, he managed to ingest half a bagel and a cup of instant black coffee. Then he checked the time to see how much longer he would have to wait until the Oscars were on.

Charlie went to the movies a lot. His friends in the motorcycle gang liked movies with a lot of car chases and gunfights, like *The Fast and the Furious* franchise. Charlie liked them too, but he also went to films with intellectual content. When the Academy Awards were handed out, he hunkered down and rooted for his favorites.

At three, he got a beer, a bag of blue corn tortilla chips, and a jar of mild salsa and turned on the E! network to watch the celebrities being interviewed as they arrived on the red carpet. Mandy Cole's interview with Meryl Streep had just ended when a handsome, tuxedo-clad gentleman with professionally coifed white hair and a perfect tan got out of a limousine. He reached down and extended a hand to a beautiful blonde in a tight red dress, who was wearing a diamond necklace and matching earrings that Charlie could never afford to buy.

"I see Leon Golden, who produced *Amazon*, headed our way," Mandy Cole said.

"Hi, Leon," Cole said when Golden reached her. "Am I correct when I say that this is the first time you've received an Oscar nomination?"

"It is, and we're pretty excited."

Charlie had seen the movie, which was a critically acclaimed feature about a couple who try to save their marriage by taking a wildlife cruise to a remote part of the Amazon jungle. Charlie had enjoyed the movie, but he didn't think that it should win the Oscar.

"Who is your companion, Leon?" the interviewer asked.

"Gretchen Hall, a dear friend."

Just as the interviewer was about to ask another question, two men and a woman walked down the red carpet dressed in windbreakers with the letters POLICE stenciled on them. Standing at the curb where the red carpet began were more officers. The woman held up a badge.

"Sorry to interrupt your interview, Miss Cole," the woman officer said, "but we're here to arrest Mr. Golden and Miss Hall on charges of running a sex ring that trafficked underage girls."

Hall looked sick, and Golden's tan lost a few shades.

"What are you talking about?" Golden demanded.

"Mr. Golden and Miss Hall, you are under arrest. You have the right to remain silent, and anything you say can and will be used against you in a court of law. You have the right to an attorney to represent you. If you cannot afford an attorney, one will be appointed for you at no expense."

"You're damn right I have attorneys, and they'll be suing your ass for this outrageous miscarriage of justice!" Golden yelled.

The officer seemed unaffected by the producer's outburst.

"Do you understand your rights?" she asked.

"Go fuck yourself!" Golden shouted.

Hall laid a hand on Golden's forearm. "Calm down, Leon. Everything you're saying is on TV."

"Holy shit!" Charlie said as the officers led Hall and Golden away.

CHAPTER SEVEN

CHARLIE WOKE UP AT EIGHT FORTY-FIVE ON MONDAY. HE WASN'T WOR-ried about getting to his law office late. He had no court appearances or client meetings scheduled because he only had a few clients and none with pressing business.

He rented a small office in a suite on the tenth floor of an old office building in downtown Portland. The main tenant was a ten-person firm that specialized in personal injury and family law. He paid his rent partly in cash and partly by doing work for the firm at an hourly rate.

His office was furnished with a scarred wooden desk, two client chairs, and a bookcase where he put his law school texts because the binding on the spines looked impressive. The decorations were Spartan, consisting of his college and law school diplomas and fancy documents that attested to his membership in the Oregon and Federal Bars.

Charlie was at work by a little after ten, and he'd just settled in when the receptionist told him that he had a call from the court administrator. When he hung up, he had mixed emotions. He hadn't had a new client this month, so being appointed to represent an indigent "alleged" criminal was nice, but court-appointed cases paid diddly-squat. Still, some money was better than no money, so he straightened his tie, hoisted his attaché case, and headed for the Justice Center, where newly arrested individuals were arraigned.

It only took ten minutes to get to the Justice Center from Charlie's office. It had been raining for most of the week, but the sun was out this morning. Charlie walked into the center's vaulted lobby and took the curving staircase to the next floor, where he saw Deputy District Attorney Monica Reyes in an earnest discussion with a lawyer who had a contract to represent indigent defendants. Reyes was carrying an armful of case files, and Charlie knew that one of them would have Guido Sabatini's name on its label.

Charlie had tried a case against Reyes, and she had been fair and reasonable, so he hoped they could work a deal if it turned out—as it usually did—that everyone could stop using the word *alleged* when referring to his new client.

"Hey, Monica," Charlie said when she was free.

"Oh, hi, Charlie. Who do you have?"

"Guido Sabatini. It's a burglary charge."

Monica rolled her eyes. "May God have mercy on your soul."

"You know him?"

"Oh yeah. And he's a genuine, grade A fruitcake."

Charlie frowned. "What's the story?"

Monica found Guido's file and handed copies of the indictment and several police reports to Charlie.

"First of all, his name isn't Guido Sabatini. It's Lawrence Weiss, but he refuses to answer to that name and insists on being called

Guido Sabatini. He claims he's the reincarnation of a Renaissance painter who worked with Michelangelo and Leonardo da Vinci."

Charlie grimaced. "Do you have any Xanax on you?"

Monica laughed. "You'll need something stronger by the time you finish representing Guido. I'll check with the guys in Vice and Narcotics and see if they've got anything for you in the evidence locker."

"What has Guido *allegedly* done?"

"Nothing serious. He's actually an excellent artist, and he goes to restaurants and sells the owner a painting. Then he becomes incensed if the painting isn't displayed where he wants it to be. If the owner refuses to change the painting's location, Guido 'liberates' it. This is his third offense. I just gave you the reports in the other thefts.

"In your case, the restaurant is La Bella Roma. The arresting officers didn't find the painting when they arrested Guido. I've been told that I can dismiss the case if Guido returns it. Also, he may have taken something from a safe in the owner's office. We'll want that back too."

"Okay. Let me talk to my client. What about getting him out of jail? Do you want him to post bail, or will you go with recog?"

"My boss says I can go along with a release on his own recognizance. Judge Noonan presided over Mr. Sabatini's other cases. He knows he's nuts, but he also knows that Guido will show up for court."

It was time for the arraignments to start, so Charlie followed Monica into the courtroom and took a seat in the front row.

Charlie took a seat in the front row of the spectator section. Guido's case was third on the docket, and Charlie walked through the bar of the court when it was called. Moments later, two guards brought his client into the courtroom. Guido was dressed in his floor-length caftan, and everyone stared as the guards placed him next to his court-appointed lawyer.

"I'm Charlie Webb, Mr. . . . . Should I call you Mr. Weiss or Mr. Sabatini?"

"I am Guido Sabatini!"

"Right. So, Guido, do you know what's going to happen next?"

Guido smiled. "This is not—as they say—my first rodeo. Is the nice lady at the other table going to allow my release on my own recognizance? I need to get back to my painting."

"The DA won't object if I ask the judge to let you out on your word that you'll show up for all of your court appearances."

"You have my word that I will appear when summoned."

"Good." Charlie handed Guido his card. "I had a nice talk with the DA, and I think I can get you out of your scrape with very little wear and tear."

Anthony Noonan was handling arraignments. Charlie had tried one case in the judge's court, and he thought that the judge was fair. Noonan always wore short-sleeve shirts under his robe. Every time the judge's robe fell back along his forearms, Charlie could see the tattoos Noonan had gotten in the Marine Corps. The judge had gone to college after the service, then worked his way through law school at night while driving a truck during the day. He was in his midsixties, but he still looked fit, and he had been on the bench long enough to have seen it all. When Guido was brought into the courtroom, Noonan shook his head.

"Are you ready to proceed, Mr. Webb?" Judge Noonan asked when he thought Charlie had had enough time to get acquainted with his new client.

"We are, Your Honor."

The judge looked at the prosecutor and sighed. "What has Mr. Weiss done now?"

"Sabatini, Your Honor," Guido said.

From his past experience with the defendant, the judge knew that Guido would not answer if he was called by his real name. "I forgot myself," Judge Noonan said. "What has Mr. *Sabatini* done this time?"

"He broke into La Bella Roma Italian Ristorante and . . . liberated a painting of a Venice canal he'd sold to Gretchen Hall, the owner. It's also possible that he took something from the safe in Miss Hall's office."

Charlie frowned. The name *Gretchen Hall* sounded familiar, but he couldn't remember why.

The judge turned his attention to Charlie's client.

"So, Mr. Sabatini, you're back to your old tricks."

Guido shrugged. "Unfortunately, Your Honor, great art is not appreciated in this world of TikToks and video games."

"On that, we are agreed. But your means of expressing your displeasure is—as I'm sure your attorney will explain to you— forbidden by the laws of this state. How do you plead to the charge?"

"Mr. Sabatini pleads not guilty, Your Honor," Charlie said. "Miss Reyes and I discussed the matter of release, and she has no objection to Mr. Sabatini being released on his own recognizance."

"Is that correct, Miss Reyes?"

"Yes, Your Honor."

The judge looked Guido in the eyes. "I'm going to let you out on your own recognizance, Mr. Sabatini. I do this reluctantly, given your history."

"Thank you, Your Honor." Guido smiled. "You have always shown me mercy, and it would give me great pleasure to gift you a painting of one of the saints, whose merciful actions you personify."

"I'm sure one of your paintings would brighten my courtroom. Unfortunately, I am not allowed to accept gifts from litigants. And given your track record, I would be afraid that you would break into the courthouse and 'liberate' it."

"I assure you, I would not."

"Mr. Sabatini, please stop doing what you're doing," the judge said. "You are a nuisance, and you are trying my patience. If I find you back here again, I will lock you up and set a very high bail."

The judge turned to his bailiff. "Please call the next case."

"You'll be processed out pretty soon," Charlie told Guido. "I'm going to my office. Come over when you get out. I'll have time to read the police reports by then, and I'll have a better handle on your case."

Guido smiled. "Thank you for your excellent assistance, Mr. Webb. I look forward to discussing how Miss Hall offended me and my wonderful portrait of a moonlit canal in Venice."

WHEN CHARLIE GOT BACK TO HIS OFFICE, HE TOLD THE RECEPTIONIST that Jesus Christ would be asking for him sometime in the afternoon and she was to treat him like any other client. Then he went into his office and read the reports of Guido's other encounters with the law. An hour and a half later, the receptionist buzzed Charlie and told him that a Mr. Sabatini would like to see him.

Charlie went into the waiting area and escorted Guido down the hall to his office. When he entered, Guido looked around the room.

"You could use some art to brighten your office," Guido said.

"Agreed," Charlie said. "Have a seat."

Guido sat in one of the client chairs and beamed at Charlie.

"The DA gave me the file for your other cases, and they have photographs of the paintings you . . . liberated. They're really good."

"Of course. I had the finest teachers. Have you been to Italia and seen the works of da Vinci and Michelangelo?"

"Uh, not yet."

Guido smiled. "You must go."

"Yeah, it's on my list. So, Guido, I'd love to see the painting of the canal in Venice that you sold to Miss Hall. Why don't we go get it and bring it back to her so we can get your case dismissed?"

Guido stiffened. "I will not return my painting to a Neander-thal who thinks so little of it that she hides it away where no one can see it."

"If you don't return the painting, you'll go to jail."

Guido smiled patiently at Charlie like someone with a secret. "I don't think so, Mr. Webb. I am certain that Miss Hall will ask for my case to be dismissed if you tell her that I will return my paint-ing and everything else to her, if she agrees in writing to hang it in the dining room of La Bella Roma Italian Ristorante and asks the district attorney to drop her charges."

Charlie frowned. "What is 'everything else'?"

Guido's smile widened. "That, as they say, is for me to know and you to find out." He stood up. "And now I must return to my studio. My muse calls to me."

"But, Mr. Sabatini . . ."

Guido stopped at the door and smiled. "I know you will do your best, Mr. Webb, but I have another counselor who protects me."

Charlie frowned. "You hired a lawyer?"

"No. God does not require a fee to protect his children."

And with that parting shot, Guido Sabatini walked out. Charlie watched him go, puzzled by Guido's belief that Gretchen Hall would drop the charges, dying to know what else Guido had stolen from La Bella Roma and wondering why Hall's name sounded familiar.

Monica Reyes was right. Guido was a grade A fruitcake. He decided that he would take up her offer to get him powerful drugs from the police evidence locker. He was going to need them as long as Guido was his client.

CHAPTER EIGHT

CHARLIE SPENT AN HOUR ON A DIVORCE HE WAS HANDLING FOR HIS cousin. When he was finished, his thoughts returned to Guido Sabatini. Who was he before he became delusional? Charlie searched the Web for "Lawrence Weiss." Several individuals popped up, but one stood out.

Lawrence Weiss majored in mathematics at Cal Berkeley, where he earned a bachelor's degree, and Stanford, where he had earned his master's. Weiss had used his mathematical abilities to amass a small fortune in casinos around the country until he had been banned for counting cards. While working on his Ph.D., he had been hired by the University of Oregon, and he had been on its faculty until he quit in the middle of the term after claiming that he was a reincarnation of a painter who had trained in Renaissance Italy with Michelangelo and Leonardo da Vinci.

Charlie stared at the monitor and wondered what had caused Guido's break from reality. Charlie decided that he would probably never know what it was if he could convince Gretchen Hall to agree to hang the Venice painting in the dining room of La Bella Roma. If that happened, Guido's case would disappear, and he wouldn't have to do any more work on it.

He looked at the police report in the Bella Roma case and found the phone number for the restaurant. Salvatore Borelli picked up after three rings.

"La Bella Roma Italian Ristorante. How can I help you?"

"Hi. My name is Charlie Webb, and I'm the attorney representing Guido Sabatini, the guy who took your painting."

"Condolences. That guy is some piece of work."

"Yeah, I can see why you'd say that. I'd like to talk to Gretchen Hall so I can get the painting back to her."

There was dead air for a moment.

When Borelli spoke, he sounded nervous. "Miss Hall isn't in Oregon. She's in LA."

"When will she be back?"

"I'm not sure."

"Can you give her my number and ask her to call me? I think we can settle the problem pretty quickly."

"Sure. I'll tell her you called."

Charlie recited his number and ended the call. He decided that there was nothing more he could do in Guido's case until he talked to Gretchen Hall. He put the file on his desk and pulled up the draft of the memorandum in support of the motion to suppress that was due Friday. Then he froze. Gretchen Hall had been arrested on the red carpet along with the guy who produced *Amazon*!

Charlie began surfing the Web for information about the case against Leon Golden and Gretchen Hall. It didn't take him long to find a video of a press conference that had been held shortly after the arrests and to recognize a familiar face. Bridget Fournier was standing at a podium in the Multnomah County district attorney's office in Portland.

During the press conference, Fournier was vague about the facts of the sex trafficking case, so Charlie didn't know a lot about it when she stepped away from the microphone. He did learn that a man named Yuri Makarov had also been arrested. Charlie frowned as something occurred to him. Guido seemed awfully confident that Gretchen Hall was going to drop the charges against him. Why was he so sure? Suddenly, Charlie had an overpowering desire to know what Guido Sabatini had stolen from the safe in Hall's office.

PART TWO
THE FLASH

CHAPTER NINE

AFTER SHE WAS ARRESTED, AND AS SOON AS SHE WAS GIVEN ACCESS to a phone, Gretchen Hall called Anita Bishop, her attorney at Prentice, Newberry, and Scott. Before joining Prentice, Newberry, and Scott, Anita had spent four years in the Multnomah County district attorney's office and had prosecuted property theft crimes in the same unit as Bridget Fournier. Fournier had agreed to let Gretchen out on bail if she waived extradition to Portland to face her charges. Gretchen Hall had arrived in Portland the day after Bishop flew to LA.

Bishop was conferring with her client in the hall outside the courtroom in Portland, where Gretchen was going to be arraigned. Leon Golden and Yuri Makarov, Golden's bodyguard, were conferring with their legal team at the other end of the corridor from Hall and Bishop.

When Bridget Fournier saw that Golden, Makarov, and their legal team weren't paying attention to her, Hall, or Bishop, she walked next to Hall's lawyer.

"Call me after court if you want Hall to get first dibs on a favorable deal," she whispered before turning her back on Bishop and walking into the courtroom.

FOR MANY YEARS, THE MULTNOMAH COUNTY DISTRICT ATTORNEY'S office had been located in the upper floors of the old Multnomah County Courthouse, an eight-story, gray concrete building that occupied a block in the middle of downtown Portland. The courthouse had been constructed between 1909 and 1914, and it had been abandoned in 2020 after a new, modern, seismically safer building was constructed near the west end of the Hawthorne Bridge. The new location gave visitors and the courthouse staff a view of boats cruising the Willamette River and the magnificent snow-covered slopes of the Cascade Mountain Range. The district attorneys now shared the view.

At eight in the morning on the day after the arraignment, Gretchen Hall and Anita Bishop sat on one side of a long conference table in the Multnomah County district attorney's office. On the other side were Bridget Fournier and Timothy Chang, another senior DA. There were floor-to-ceiling windows behind the deputy DAs, but neither Gretchen nor her attorney paid any attention to the view.

Bridget looked directly at Gretchen. "I'll give your lawyer a package with the discovery in our case when our meeting is over, Miss Hall. Now, I'm going to lay out our case so you'll have an idea of what you're facing if you decide to go to trial.

"Several women have testified in a grand jury that you lured them to Leon Golden's estate with promises that he would give them roles in one of his films. Some of these women were underage. The estate is isolated, and there were guards with dogs patrolling the grounds.

"The women will testify that they were shown to a bedroom by a very large man, who we have identified as Yuri Makarov, Mr. Golden's assistant and bodyguard. Makarov told the girls that they had to have sex with the men who were financing the movie in order to get the part. When they refused, Makarov showed them a film in which a masked man raped and killed a young girl. He told the girls that they would not be allowed to leave if they didn't submit to his demands. When Makarov left them, he locked them in.

"The girls testified that they were very frightened and had sex with several men because they believed that they would be killed if they didn't. After they had sex with the men, they were paid off and allowed to leave. Mr. Makarov told them that they would be killed if they revealed what happened at the estate. They were also told that no one would believe them, because Golden had judges and police on his payroll.

"Two of these girls met up by accident afterward and decided to go to the police. We've been investigating their claims and have found other witnesses."

"Who are these girls?" Anita asked.

"Right now, they are all Jane Does. We have a court order protecting their identities because of the threats that were made, but you won't need to know their identities if Miss Hall agrees to testify for the State. I'm offering her this chance for a lighter sentence. I'd like the testimony of an insider to bolster our case against Leon Golden, and I am particularly interested in a list of the men who had sex with these women and a copy of the snuff film."

"What does Miss Hall get in exchange for her testimony?" Anita asked.

"I'll need a proffer before I can decide. Why don't you read the discovery, talk to your client, and get back to me. But don't wait too long."

Hall and Bishop left the conference room.

"Let's go to our office and review the discovery," Anita said.

"Can it wait?" Gretchen asked. "I'm physically and mentally exhausted. I don't think I can concentrate. Can you have a copy of the discovery sent to my house? I'll call you when I've read it."

"Okay," Anita said. "But get back to me as soon as you can."

Gretchen wasn't lying about being exhausted, but there was something she had to do before heading home. The ride to La Bella Roma was short, and she arrived at the restaurant before it opened. The front door was locked, and Gretchen opened it with her key. She was halfway to her office when Salvatore Borelli walked out of the kitchen.

"Jesus, Gretchen! I saw the whole thing on TV. How are you doing?"

"I'm hanging on by my fingertips, Sal."

"You didn't do that stuff they say you did—grooming underage girls?"

"I'm completely innocent, and I've got great lawyers. You'll see. I'll be just fine when the smoke clears. Now, I've got to get something from my office."

"About your office. I didn't want to bother you while you were in LA, but something happened while you were away."

Gretchen stopped. "What do you mean?"

"You know the nutcase with the pictures?"

"Sabatini?"

"Yeah. He broke in a few days after you bought the Venice painting and stole it."

"What?!"

"The cops arrested him. His lawyer—a guy named Charlie Webb—called. He said you should call him so you can get the picture back. I have his number. The cops say Sabatini does this all the time—selling a painting to a restaurant, then stealing it back if he doesn't like where the owner's hanging it. He got really mad when he didn't see your painting in the dining room.

"Also, you should check your safe. It was open when I saw that the painting was gone. There's money and papers still in it, but the cops want to know if Sabatini stole anything besides the painting."

Gretchen only heard half of what Borelli said because she was on her way to her office before he finished. She flung open the door and stared at the safe, which was no longer concealed from view by a scene of a canal in Venice. Borelli followed her into her office.

Gretchen's heart was beating furiously, and she had started to perspire. She punched in the combination, swung the door of the safe open, and stared inside. Then she reached into the safe and moved objects around.

"Hey, are you okay?" Borelli asked when he saw how pale his boss was.

Gretchen turned and walked away from the safe without shutting it.

"Miss Hall . . ." Borelli started, but Gretchen waved him off.

"I need a few minutes, Sal," she said as she sat at her desk and booted up her computer. "And get me that lawyer's number."

"Sure thing," Borelli said as he backed out of the office and shut the door.

Gretchen typed "Guido Sabatini" into Google. It didn't take

long to find out that he was a painter who lived during the Renaissance, but it took a little longer to find a cross-reference to Lawrence Weiss. Minutes after she read the article, Gretchen ran out of the restaurant and drove to Leon Golden's estate.

CHAPTER TEN

ON THE DRIVE TO LEON GOLDEN'S ESTATE, GRETCHEN'S EMOTIONS ricocheted between fear and nausea. The contents of the flash drive that Guido Sabatini had stolen from her safe could send her and many other people to prison. Worse, there were some people who were featured on the drive who might decide to kill her to punish her for losing the drive or to keep her from cooperating with the police.

Golden's estate was in the middle of nowhere. To get to it, Gretchen drove down the Columbia River Gorge on I-84, then inland and across a river on a narrow bridge. The bridge connected to a private road squeezed tight by dense forestland where the canopy formed by massive trees cast the road in shadows. After a quarter of a mile, the road was blocked by a gate made of thick, black wrought iron bars that joined the two halves of a stone wall topped with razor wire. A large and intimidating guard stepped out of a sentry box and walked to the gate.

"It's Gretchen Hall, Sully. I'm here to see Leon."

"Is he expecting you?"

"Probably not. But he'll tell you to let me in if you tell him I'm here."

A few minutes later, Gretchen was driving up a narrow road through more forest. Shortly before she reached Leon's mansion, the forest gave way to well-tended lawns patrolled by men with snarling guard dogs.

Leon lived in a three-story redbrick Georgian house with a roof of graduated slate tiles. Yuri Makarov was waiting at the front door. He was in his forties, but he still looked like he could compete at light heavyweight, the weight class he'd boxed in before Leon hired him. Makarov walked over to Gretchen when she got out of her car.

"Mr. Golden's lawyers told him that he's not supposed to talk to you."

"I got the same warning. What our lawyers don't know is that a lunatic named Guido Sabatini broke into my wall safe in La Bella Roma and stole a flash drive with the names of your guests and a copy of a certain movie. Tell him that, Yuri, then tell me what he says."

Gretchen waited at the front door, but she didn't have to wait long.

"He'll see you," Makarov said.

Gretchen followed Leon's bodyguard down a hall to a wood-paneled study lined with bookcases that looked out on a side lawn. She started to say something when she walked inside, but Golden held up his hand.

"I know you met with the DA," Golden said.

"You spied on me?"

"And you didn't tell me you were hobnobbing with the people who want to put me in prison. So, before we talk, I want you to strip so I can see if you're wearing a wire."

"Screw you, Leon."

Golden shrugged. "It wouldn't be the first time I've seen you naked."

Gretchen flushed. "Oh, for fuck's sake. But I want him out of the room."

"No problem."

Makarov left and shut the door.

Leon watched Gretchen strip. Then he made her turn around.

"You've still got it, Gretchen," Leon said as he admired Gretchen's body.

"Grow up," Gretchen said as she dressed. "Now, are you ready to get serious? Because we could have a big problem."

Leon's face darkened when Gretchen told him about the theft of the flash drive.

"Are you going to explain how this lunatic got into your safe?"

"Sabatini's real name is Lawrence Weiss, and he's an artist. I bought a painting from him, and I paid in cash I took from my safe. He was in my office when I punched in the combination.

"Weiss is also some kind of math genius. He can count cards, and he won a lot of money in casinos before they caught on and banned him. I don't know how he did it, but I'm betting that he memorized my combination when I got his money from the safe."

"Jesus, Gretchen, how stupid can you be!"

"I never saw him as a threat, Leon, and calling me names won't get the flash drive back. So, let's focus on that."

"What do you suggest?"

"Sal told me that Sabatini's lawyer called. I have his number."

"Call him. See what he wants."

Hall found the number in her purse and dialed.

"Charles Webb's office," a male answered.

"I'd like to talk to Mr. Webb. Tell him Gretchen Hall, the owner of La Bella Roma, is calling."

"Oh, hi, Miss Hall. This is Charles. Thanks for calling."

"I understand that you're representing Guido Sabatini."

"I am, and I think I can get you back the painting and the other objects he took."

"I see. How would you do that?"

"Mr. Sabatini only wants to have his painting displayed where everyone can see it. If you agree in writing to hang it in the restaurant's dining room and tell the DA to drop the charges, he'll return it."

"That shouldn't be a problem. You mentioned some other objects. What was he referring to?"

"Honestly, I don't know. I asked, but he wouldn't tell me. But he'll definitely return them if you agree to hang the painting in the dining room. That's all he's interested in."

"That isn't a problem, and I'll have no reason to see him prosecuted if I get the painting back. So, how do we do this?"

"Mr. Sabatini doesn't want to come downtown because that means he can't be painting. He wants to do everything at his farm. I'll give you the address. Let's meet there at noon. I'll bring the paperwork."

"That sounds good. I'll see you tomorrow."

When Gretchen ended the call, she turned to Golden.

"Sabatini will return the painting and everything else if I agree to hang his painting in the dining room at La Bella Roma and drop the charges against him. I'm going to his farm tomorrow at noon."

"Did the lawyer know what Sabatini took in addition to the painting?"

"He told me that Sabatini wouldn't tell him."

"That's a relief. That means that Sabatini is our only threat."

"Don't do anything stupid, Leon. This guy is nuts. All he cares about is his artwork. If he wanted to blackmail me, he'd have made his move already. If we're lucky, I'll have the flash drive tomorrow."

"I'll wait to hear from you. Hopefully, we'll all be breathing easier by tomorrow afternoon."

Golden walked Gretchen to her car. As soon as she left, he returned to his study and took a burner phone out of his desk and called Max Unger.

"We have a potential problem, Max," Golden said.

"I hope you or Hall aren't the problem."

"No, no. I'd never sell you out."

"What about Hall? She met with the DA. They offered her a deal."

"How do you know that?"

"I know a lot of things."

"Gretchen isn't going to cooperate with the DA. It's something else entirely."

Golden told Unger about the theft at La Bella Roma.

"This fruitcake has the flash drive?" Unger asked. He sounded panicky.

"Gretchen assures me that this guy is nuts and hasn't tried to use what's on the flash drive for blackmail. Hopefully, she'll have everything back tomorrow so you can relax."

"Don't tell me to relax. You know what will happen if the DA gets that drive."

"Of course I do."

"Where is Sabatini's farm?"

"Why do you want to know?"

"Just give me the address."

"Don't do anything until you hear from me," Golden said as soon as he'd told Unger where Hall was going to meet the artist.

"I'll do what I think is best," Unger said. Then he disconnected.

CHAPTER ELEVEN

GUIDO HAD TRADED HIS CAFTAN FOR A PAINT-STAINED SWEATSHIRT and jeans, and he was painting a portrait of Saint Francis of Assisi when he heard a car drive up to his barn. He walked into the yard and saw a man dressed in pressed jeans, a blue shirt, and a tweed jacket with leather elbow patches walking toward him. The man was average height and had a slender build. His ginger hair, mustache, and goatee looked like they had been cut and trimmed by a professional.

"Mr. Sabatini?" the man inquired.

"Sì."

"I'm Rene LaTour. I just flew in from San Francisco, and I would be grateful if you could spare me a few moments of your time."

Guido couldn't think of any reason anyone would fly from San Francisco to see him, so he led LaTour into the barn to solve the mystery.

LaTour walked over to Guido's easel and studied the work in progress.

"This is really good, Mr. Sabatini," LaTour said. "And your exceptional paintings are the reason I wanted to meet with you."

"Yes?"

"I'll get right to the point. I represent a wealthy art collector who has been following your case. He's seen photographs of your artwork on your website, and he has been very impressed. He wants to purchase several of your paintings."

"Who is your client, signor?"

LaTour smiled. "He prefers to remain anonymous, and he trusts me to select the paintings for him. He is willing to pay good money for them."

"You have my attention. How much money are we talking about?"

"In the neighborhood of fifteen thousand dollars for each painting."

Guido nodded. Then he frowned. "I may be interested, but tell me. You say you represent a private collector. Will he be keeping my paintings in his residence, where no one can see them?"

LaTour smiled. "We know that you want to have as many people as possible admire your artistry. I have a gallery, and we plan to display your work so everyone can admire it."

Guido smiled. "Ah, *bene*. Do you wish to see my paintings?"

"Of course."

LaTour spent the next hour in the stalls where Guido kept his finished work. By the time he was through, LaTour had settled on six paintings he said he would recommend that his client purchase and had taken a photograph of each of them.

"I'm going to return to San Francisco tonight, and I'll call you tomorrow after I confer with my client."

"I look forward to hearing whether your client appreciates what I have accomplished."

"I'm certain he will. And now, before I go, there's one more article we would like to purchase."

"Oh?"

"You're charged with liberating a painting of a Venice canal from La Bella Roma restaurant."

"Yes."

"I understand that you also took a flash drive from Miss Hall's safe."

Guido stopped smiling.

"My client will pay another sum for the flash drive, which will be in excess of what he will pay you for your exceptional paintings."

Guido took a moment to respond. "It is obvious that you have no interest in my work, Signor LaTour. It is this other item that you believe I have that has brought you to my farm, is it not?"

"My client does admire your paintings, but he has a personal reason for acquiring the flash drive, and he is willing to meet your price, if it is within reason."

"And if it is not or I refuse to part with this drive—which, by the way, I do not say I possess—what then?"

"You don't want to go there, Mr. Sabatini. Let me make this clear. My client prefers to pay you for your trouble, but it can be very dangerous to turn down his offer."

Guido nodded. "Thank you for your honesty. But I must decline your offer. And now I want you to leave so I can return to my painting."

"Don't make a rash decision, Mr. Sabatini. I'll call before I fly home. Think about our offer and the downside of rejecting it."

LaTour made certain that he was out of sight of the farm before he parked on the side of the road and made a call.

"I just left Sabatini. He caught on right away."

"I'm not surprised," Max Unger said. "The guy's no dummy. What did he say?"

"As soon as he realized that we wanted the flash drive and didn't care about his paintings, he closed down."

"He wouldn't sell the drive?"

"I'm calling him later, after he's had time to think. I'll let you know how that goes."

BRAD AND BRENT ATKINS WORKED AT THE LOADING DOCK AT A BIG-BOX store.

"Hey, did you see this?" asked Brad, who had been reading the local news while they were on their lunch break.

"See what?"

Brad showed his brother a photograph of a man who looked like Jesus Christ walking out of a courtroom.

"No. Why should I care?"

"Doesn't he look familiar?"

"Well, yeah. I saw him every time Mom took us to church."

"No, you idiot. Picture him in jeans and a plaid shirt, wearing a Mariners baseball cap."

Brent leaned into the screen and stared. Then he straightened up. "It's the dude who took our money."

"That's what I think."

"Why is he in court?" Brent asked.

"It says his name is Lawrence Weiss, but he's an artist who calls himself Guido Sabatini. He's charged with breaking into an Italian restaurant and stealing a painting he sold to the owner."

"Look him up. See if they say where he lives."

Brad did an internet search on his phone.

"Holy shit," he said when he was through.

"What?"

"Weiss is a math genius, and he's been banned from all the big casinos for card counting. It sounds like he's a World Series of Poker–level player."

"Motherfucker," Brent swore. "I knew something was off about that guy. He's got no business playing in a local game like the one Frank runs at the gun store."

"I don't get this deal with the Jesus outfit," Brad said. "It sounds like he has a screw loose."

"Does it say where he lives?" Brent asked.

"Yeah. It's a farm out in the country. Why?"

"I'm gonna pay that asshole a visit and get our money back."

"I don't think that's such a good idea. He was packing at the poker game."

"He got the drop on us. That won't happen again."

"I think you should forget it. He didn't rob us. He's just a real good poker player."

"No, Brad. Weiss is a major leaguer who took advantage of two dumb shits who were just trying to have some fun."

"Please don't do anything stupid."

Brent was quiet for a minute. Then he smiled. "Lunch break's over. Let's get back to work."

"Brent, leave it alone."

Brent got up and walked back to the loading dock without answering.

GUIDO SABATINI HAD WATCHED THE MOVIE ON THE FLASH DRIVE HE'D taken from Gretchen Hall's safe, and he'd found it disturbing. When it started, a beautiful blond girl was sitting on a bed in a small room. Guido thought that she looked very young, possibly just in her teens. The door opened, and the girl looked very anxious. Her anxiety increased when a man in a mask walked in. There wasn't any sound, but the man said something, and the girl scuttled to the back of the bed, only stopping when her back was against the wall. The man attacked his victim, ripping her clothes and hitting her when she resisted. Then he raped the girl and strangled her.

Guido felt sick when the film ended. He knew that he should show it to the police, but he had no intention of turning it over to the authorities. If he did, he would become a witness in a court proceeding, and that would mean time away from his painting. That was why he had decided to return everything to Gretchen Hall once she agreed to hang his painting in La Bella Roma's dining room. That didn't mean that he was oblivious to the precarious position he'd put himself in when he stole the flash drive from the safe.

Guido's IQ was comfortably above the minimum it took to be considered a genius. He knew that just because he had decided that he would not be a threat to the people involved in the sex trafficking ring didn't mean that those same people would not see him as a problem. Rene LaTour's veiled threat had supported his conclusion that dangerous people wanted the drive.

There had been a time when Guido's earnings from his poker and blackjack exploits had made him wealthy. These exploits had also made him the object of threats from the people who ran the casinos he had scammed and some shady individuals who had resented being cleaned out in backroom poker games that were contested in the shadows. When he was still able to afford it, Guido had purchased the farm and installed a top-of-the-line security system.

As soon as Guido watched the film, he started leaving on lights that operated on a timer in his house and sleeping in a stall in his barn that housed the security camera feeds. Guido was not a pacifist. Renaissance painters like Caravaggio were not averse to violence. But Guido believed that God protected him. How else to explain the many times he had not suffered consequences when he'd liberated his paintings from ungrateful purchasers?

On the evening before he was supposed to meet Gretchen Hall, he was awakened by a motion sensor on the periphery of his property. Guido turned to the pictures his security cameras were sending, and he saw a man he recognized as one of the brothers from the gun store poker game sneaking through the woods toward his farm.

Guido sighed. He took out his gun and was preparing to head off the fool before anyone got hurt when he saw a masked figure dressed in black clothing closing on the brother. They didn't look like they were together. Guido found this disturbing.

Guido had an escape route that started at the back of the barn. He grabbed his portfolio, the Venice canal painting, and the flash drive and hurried to the car he'd parked on a back road.

CHAPTER TWELVE

CHARLIE WEBB HAD FORCED HIMSELF TO BE ALL BUSINESS WHEN Gretchen Hall called, but it felt weird talking to someone who had been arrested on the red carpet at the Oscars for sex trafficking. It was like getting a call from a celebrity, even if the cause of the person's notoriety wasn't a good thing. Charlie reminded himself that Guido's case had nothing to do with sex trafficking, so Charlie knew better than to bring up Gretchen's case while they were finalizing the deal that would keep his client out of jail.

Charlie drove into the yard in front of Guido's farmhouse at eleven thirty, because he wanted to talk to his client before Gretchen Hall arrived at noon. Charlie knocked on the farmhouse door and waited for Guido to open it. After a reasonable amount of time, he knocked again and shouted Guido's name. When there was still no response, he tried the door and found that it was open. Charlie walked into the entryway and called out, "Hello, Guido?" There was still no answer, and he was going to call again when he walked past the living room. It looked like a tornado had ripped through it.

Charlie's instinct was to flee, but he stopped after a backward step. Guido could be injured. Charlie took a deep breath and began to walk through the house. Every room was a portrait of devastation, and Guido wasn't in any of them.

Charlie left the house and was headed toward the barn when a car drove into the front yard. It stopped, and Gretchen Hall and Yuri Makarov got out.

"Are you Gretchen Hall?" Charlie asked.

Gretchen nodded. "And I assume you're Mr. Webb."

"Yeah. Call me Charlie. Thanks for coming."

Charlie thought that Makarov looked scary. He was almost as big as Charlie but constructed of solid muscle, and an aura of menace surrounded him.

"Who's your companion?" Charlie asked.

"Yuri Makarov is a friend."

Charlie remembered reading that a man named Yuri Makarov had been arrested in connection with the sex trafficking scheme.

"So, where is Mr. Sabatini?"

"Good question. He isn't in the house, and it looks like it's been searched. I'm going to see if he's in the barn."

When Charlie walked into the barn, he saw Guido's easel lying on its side and his paints strewn across the floor. Makarov walked to the first stall, and Charlie followed. The video monitors connected to the security system had been smashed and the wiring ripped out. Someone had taken a knife to Guido's mattress.

"He's not here," Makarov said after he searched the rest of the barn.

"Neither is the painting," Charlie said. "If he got away, he has it."

Gretchen's gut was in a knot, but she kept calm. "Let me know if Mr. Sabatini gets in touch," she said.

"Definitely," Charlie said as he handed Gretchen his card. "Do you think I should call the police?"

Gretchen did not want the police anywhere near Guido.

"What would you say? Guido is crazy. He might have done this himself. He'll probably call you, and we can finish our business."

"Point taken," Charlie said. "I'm sorry you were inconvenienced."

"No problem." She turned to Yuri. "Let's go back to town."

Charlie got in his car and followed Gretchen to the highway. Guido was nuts, so Charlie could see him running amok in his house, but destroying his easel and his paints . . . ? No way. Guido lived to paint. That meant that somebody else was looking for the items Guido took from the safe. It also meant that Guido was in danger.

CHAPTER THIRTEEN

GRETCHEN DIDN'T SPEAK DURING THE DRIVE HOME BECAUSE SHE WAS trying to figure out who had ransacked Guido's house and barn. She didn't think Leon had sent anyone. He'd have no reason to, because he thought Gretchen was going to retrieve the flash drive with the list and the movie. Did Leon tell someone where Sabatini lived? That was a possibility, and she was determined to ask him as soon as she was alone.

When she was almost at her house, her phone rang. She didn't recognize the number.

"Yeah?" she said.

"If you want the flash drive, meet me in Tryon Creek state park at eleven o'clock tonight with fifty thousand dollars."

"Who is this?"

"I'm the person who can bring your world crashing down."

Gretchen took a deep breath to calm herself. "The park is big," she said. "Where should I meet you?"

The caller gave Hall directions and disconnected.

"Who was that?" Makarov asked.

Hall told Yuri Makarov what had just happened.

"Did you recognize the voice?"

"The caller was using a device that made it impossible to tell if it was a man or a woman."

"You think the caller has the flash drive?"

"Sabatini might have an accomplice."

"What do you want to do?"

"I have to go."

"Can you get the money?"

"We'll go to my bank. It shouldn't be a problem."

"Are you just going to walk into the park?" Makarov asked.

"Of course not. I want you out there as soon as you drop me at home. We're supposed to meet on the other side of a bridge, a short distance from one of the roadside parking lots. Find a good vantage point to watch the place where I'm supposed to bring the money."

"Then what?"

"Grab the son of a bitch, but don't kill him. We need him alive so we can get the drive back."

GRETCHEN PARKED AND SAT IN HER CAR FOR A MINUTE TO GATHER HER courage. A sliver of a moon was hidden behind dark clouds, and it was pitch black in the park. In a few minutes, she was going into that park with $50,000 to meet someone who might try to kill her. Gretchen had never done anything remotely like this, and she was sick to her stomach. She took a quick look at her cell phone. They had agreed that Makarov would call her if he had the blackmailer, but Makarov had not called.

Gretchen did some deep breathing to calm herself, grabbed the suitcase with the money, and got out of the car. She switched on a flashlight and cast its beam on the trail that led into the park from the lot. A cold breeze swept through the trees, and she started every time leaves rustled or a nocturnal animal slithered through the underbrush.

Shortly after leaving the lot, she saw the bridge. She swung the beam of her flashlight back and forth, but all she saw were trees and bushes. When she was at the meeting point, she turned off the light so she wouldn't be a target. She knew Makarov was lurking somewhere in the dark, and she hoped he would protect her.

Gretchen looked at her watch. It was just past eleven. She turned in a circle, looking for the person she was supposed to meet. She had just faced the bridge when she heard a branch snap behind her.

CHAPTER FOURTEEN

AFTER HE RETURNED TO HIS OFFICE, CHARLIE WAITED FOR GUIDO TO call, but there were no calls from his client by the time he went home. Charlie didn't sleep well that night. He kept thinking about Guido. Was he safe? Did the person or persons who had ransacked Guido's house and barn have him? Had they killed him?

Charlie tossed and turned and woke up at six fifteen, groggy and with a head full of cotton. He tried and failed to get back to sleep and finally gave up.

It was rare for Charlie to be one of the first lawyers to arrive at the suite in the morning, and the dark hallways seemed spooky. He settled behind his desk and leafed through the files in his active cases. He didn't have many, and there wasn't much to do in them. That was depressing, so he distracted himself by reading the sports news on his phone until the receptionist buzzed him to inform him that two detectives wanted to talk to him. Charlie frowned. Could they be there about Guido? There was only one way to find out.

A slim woman with curly blond hair, dressed in a gray pant-suit and yellow blouse, walked toward Charlie when he entered the waiting room. A thickset African-American man in black slacks, a black turtleneck shirt, and a blazer followed her.

"I'm Sally Blaisedale, and this is Gordon Rawls," the woman said as she flashed her badge and credentials. "We're detectives with Portland Homicide."

"Homicide? Is this about Guido Sabatini? Uh, his real name is Lawrence Weiss."

The detectives looked at each other for a second, then back at Charlie.

"Why do you think this is about Mr. Weiss?"

"I'm representing him. He stole a painting from a restaurant. He was supposed to give it back to the owner yesterday, but when she met me at his farm, he wasn't there, and his house and barn had been ransacked."

"Did you report this to the police?"

Charlie flushed with embarrassment. "Guido—Mr. Weiss—is mentally ill, and I wasn't certain that he didn't wreck his own place."

"Who was the owner of the painting?" Detective Rawls asked.

"Gretchen Hall. She's the owner of La Bella Roma restaurant. The DA said she'd drop the charges if Guido gave back the painting. Miss Hall didn't think we should call the police either."

"Was Miss Hall alone when she came to Mr. Sabatini's farm?"

"No. She had a driver."

"Do you remember his name?"

"Yuri Makarov."

"We'd like you to come with us, Mr. Webb," Rawls said.

"Where?"

"Tryon Creek park. That's where a runner found Gretchen Hall's body. It was covered by a painting of Saint Francis of Assisi. The painter signed the painting. Want to guess who he is?"

TRYON CREEK STATE NATURAL AREA WAS 658 ACRES OF SECOND-GROWTH forest fifteen minutes from downtown Portland. The park had eight miles of hiking trails, a boardwalk over wetlands, and eight bridges. The detectives drove down a road that ran along the side of the park and pulled into a parking area near one of the trailheads. Charlie recognized the car that Yuri Makarov and Gretchen Hall had driven to the farm. There was a lot of activity around it.

Charlie had been very nervous during the drive in the police car, and he felt dizzy as he followed the detectives along a trail that led into the park. Detective Blaisedale told him that Gretchen Hall's body was lying in the underbrush a few feet from one of the bridges and a quarter of a mile in from the parking area. When he crossed the bridge and got his first glimpse of Gretchen's body, he turned his head so he would only see the dead body out of the corner of his eye. The police had left the body the way it had been found, and Guido's painting covered her torso, but Charlie could see the bullet hole in Hall's forehead and the blood that had spattered across her face.

Charlie had to use all his willpower to keep from throwing up.

"Are you okay?" Blaisedale asked.

"I've never seen a dead body before, except my grandmother at her funeral. And she hadn't been . . ." Charlie licked his lips. "You know."

"I do, and you did better than I did when I saw my first murder victim. Do you want some water?"

Charlie nodded. The detective held out a plastic bottle, and Charlie sipped from it.

"When you're ready, we'd like you to look at Miss Hall and tell us if there is anything different about her from what you saw yesterday. Tell me when you're ready."

Charlie took another drink. Then he took a deep breath. Blaisedale led him to the corpse and pulled back the painting. Charlie looked below Hall's neck so he wouldn't have to see her head again. When he'd given Hall's corpse a brief look, he turned away and noticed a handgun that was lying on the ground near Hall's body. He also noticed a suitcase lying near Hall. It was open, and he saw neatly bundled stacks of American currency in it.

"This is how Miss Hall was dressed at the farm."

"Did she have this suitcase or a gun with her?"

"If she did, I didn't see it."

"Thank you," Blaisedale said. "I hate to do this to you, but there's one more body we want you to look at."

Charlie's already ashen features grew even paler. "Who is it?"

"Yuri Makarov. Are you up to this?"

Charlie took a deep breath and nodded. Blaisedale led him down the path away from the bridge and into a thick stand of trees. Makarov was lying on his back, and there were bullet wounds in his chest and face. The ground under the back of his head was saturated with blood. Makarov's arm was outstretched, and there was a Glock lying on the ground near his right hand.

"Is this the man who drove Miss Hall to the farm?"

Charlie tried to answer, but he was too choked up to speak, so he just nodded.

Blaisedale held out the water bottle and took Charlie's arm. "You did great, Mr. Webb. Let's get you out of here."

Blaisedale waited until they'd crossed the bridge to ask Charlie the question that she'd wanted to ask all morning. "Can you tell us where to find Mr. Weiss, Charlie?"

"Honestly, no. After seeing what happened at his farm, I'm really worried. Someone really trashed the place."

"Do you know why?"

"I can only guess."

"Let's hear it."

Charlie thought about everything he knew about Guido's case and decided that he wouldn't be revealing a client's confidence if he told the detectives about the "other things" Guido had taken from Gretchen Hall's office.

"Okay, now this is just speculation, but Guido didn't just take the painting of the Venice canal. He told me to tell Miss Hall that he would return the painting and some other things he'd taken if she would ask the DA to drop the charges."

"What other things?"

"He would never tell me, but I know that Miss Hall and Mr. Makarov were arrested for sex trafficking, and I've wondered if the items had some connection to that because Guido seemed pretty certain that Hall would drop the charges."

"You negotiated with Hall, right?" Blaisedale asked.

"Yes, but she never told me what the other things were."

"Okay. Thank you. I know this hasn't been easy. Do you want to go home or to your office?"

"Home, I guess."

Blaisedale and Rawls handed Charlie their cards.

"Call us if Mr. Weiss gets in touch."

"I don't know if I can do that. I'm still his lawyer. But I'll try to get him to talk to you." Charlie shook his head. "I just can't see him doing this. And covering the body with one of his paintings . . . That looks like a frame. Guido is passionate about only one thing—his art—and I can't see him desecrating a painting by using it to cover the body of someone he'd murdered."

CHAPTER FIFTEEN

CHARLIE HADN'T SLEPT MUCH THE NIGHT BEFORE HE WAS TAKEN TO SEE Gretchen Hall's corpse. He hardly slept at all the evening after the trip to the state park, tossing and turning into the wee hours as he wondered what Guido had gotten himself into. When he did fall asleep, all his dreams were terrifying.

In the morning, he went to work, hoping that Guido would call. As soon as he walked into his office, he had a feeling that something was off. He had won a drunk-driving case for a client who lived in Hawaii. Along with his check, the client had sent him a shark's jaw as a joke. Charlie used it as a paperweight, and he distinctly remembered putting it dead center on top of a pile of reports in a case that was sitting on a corner of his desk. The jaw was off center.

A metal filing cabinet with four drawers stood against one wall. Charlie was certain that all the drawers had been completely shut when he'd left his office, but the bottom drawer was not shut as tightly as the others. He opened each drawer and looked at his files. They were in place.

Did someone search his office, or was he hypersensitive because of his lack of sleep and the shock of seeing two dead bodies? Before he could reach a conclusion, the receptionist buzzed him.

"There's a Mr. Sabatini on line two," she said.

"Guido, where are you?" Charlie asked as soon as they were connected.

"I am in the Multnomah County jail."

"What are you doing there?" Charlie asked, afraid that he knew the answer.

"I have been arrested for murder, and I would like to discuss this with you."

THE MULTNOMAH COUNTY JAIL WAS ON THE FOURTH THROUGH TENTH floors of the Justice Center, where Guido Sabatini had been arraigned on his burglary charge. Charlie showed his bar card to the officer in the reception area before walking through a metal detector and taking an elevator to the floor where there were rooms for attorneys to have contact visits with their clients.

Charlie left the elevator and found himself in a narrow concrete hall. There was a button affixed to a thick metal door at one end of the hall. Moments after he pressed it, electronic locks snapped in place. A corrections officer opened the door and led Charlie into another narrow corridor that ran in front of three contact visiting rooms. Charlie could see into them through shatterproof windows. The officer opened the door to the first visiting room, and Charlie entered a concrete rectangle furnished with two plastic chairs and a table that was secured to the floor by metal bolts.

Moments after Charlie sat down, a second metal door in the wall opposite the window opened, and a guard led Guido into the room. Guido was dressed in an orange jumpsuit instead of his caftan, but he still flashed a warm smile at his lawyer and looked completely at ease.

"It is so good of you to meet with me, Charlie," Guido said as he took the seat across from his attorney.

"I want to be clear that I won't be your lawyer if you're charged with killing Gretchen Hall and Yuri Makarov."

"Why won't you help me if these are the charges?"

"Because I'm not competent to handle a murder case. That's a specialty. The only contact I've had with crimes of violence is a bar fight I handled two years ago, and I lost that case. But don't worry. The court will appoint a lawyer with experience in homicide cases."

"I don't want another lawyer. I trust you."

"I appreciate that, but I don't think any judge will appoint me in a double homicide. They'd know I'm not competent to handle a murder case."

Guido shrugged. "If I can't have you as my lawyer, I will represent myself."

"That's ridiculous. You don't know the first thing about being a lawyer."

"I will read books."

"Look, Guido, I know you have a genius IQ, but being good at math doesn't mean you know the first thing about handling a murder case."

Guido smiled, stood up, and rang for the guard.

"I have made my decision. Thank you for taking the time from your busy day to visit me."

CHAPTER SIXTEEN

THE CALL CHARLIE HAD BEEN DREADING CAME AT TEN O'CLOCK THE next morning.

"Judge Noonan is on line one," the receptionist informed Charlie.

"Mr. Webb, you're needed in my courtroom this afternoon at two o'clock," the judge said when they were connected.

"Uh, what for?"

"Mr. Weiss's arraignment."

"Is this on those murders at Tryon Creek park?" Charlie asked, certain that he knew the answer to his question.

"Yes."

"I was afraid of that. Look, Your Honor, I already told Mr. Sabatini that I can't try a murder case. I've never handled anything that serious. You need to get someone else to represent him."

"I would have, but your client made it very clear that you have to be his lawyer. He says that he'll represent himself if you aren't appointed."

"It would be malpractice if I'm his lawyer in a murder charge."

"I'm aware of the problem, and I'll make sure you have an experienced cocounsel appointed to assist you. But you'll be doing me a big favor if you accept the appointment. Can you imagine what the trial will be like if Mr. Weiss represents himself?"

Charlie had no trouble imagining the chaos that Guido would cause if he were his own lawyer. There was an old adage that a person who represented himself had a fool for a client. Guido would be representing a lunatic.

"I don't know."

"Look, Charlie, I've seen you try a case. You do a good job. Everyone who tries murder cases had to try their first murder case without any prior experience. And I promise you I will get you a first-rate, experienced cocounsel. I don't want a conviction reversed because a defendant didn't have competent representation."

Charlie sighed. "If you promise to get me all the help I need, I'll do it. I'll need fees for investigation and experts and things I haven't even thought about."

"That won't be a problem. And I'll make sure that the DA sends you all of the discovery this morning."

THE POLICE AND THE DISTRICT ATTORNEY'S OFFICE HAD NOT BEEN SHY ABOUT publicizing Guido's arrest for the murder of two of the defendants in a major sex trafficking prosecution, and reporters swarmed in the corridor outside Judge Noonan's courtroom. None of the reporters bothered Charlie when he walked down the hall and entered the courtroom because he was a nonentity. That was just fine with him.

The courtrooms in the old courthouse featured high ceilings, ornate molding, marble Corinthian columns, and daises of polished wood. The courtrooms in the new building had none of the grandeur or historic character of the old courtrooms. They had flat, dull, brown wooden desks with clean lines that could have been bought at IKEA and were built for function, not form. Attorneys could charge laptops or phones in outlets in their counsel tables. Videos and evidence were presented to jurors on wall-mounted screens.

Judge Noonan's courtroom was packed with spectators, but Charlie had no trouble spotting detectives Blaisedale and Rawls sitting in the back row. A young woman turned toward him. Charlie guessed that she was in her late twenties, and she was so attractive Charlie had to use all his self-control to keep from staring. She smiled at Charlie. The smile puzzled him, but he realized that he had to focus on Guido's case.

Bridget Fournier was sitting at the prosecution's table.

"Hi, Bridget," Charlie said. "I didn't know you handled homicides. How come you're prosecuting Guido?"

"Maybe it's because *Mr. Weiss* murdered the person I was hoping would be my star witness in the biggest sex trafficking case in the county's history," she said as she handed him a copy of the indictment charging Lawrence Weiss, a.k.a. Guido Sabatini, with murdering Gretchen Hall and Yuri Makarov.

"Whoa. Hold on. I've gotten to know Mr. Weiss a little, and I can't see him killing anyone. He's a fruitcake, but he's a harmless fruitcake."

"Did you read the discovery?"

"Yeah?"

"Did you read the part where two handguns were discovered in the house of your harmless fruitcake when it was searched pursuant to a warrant authorized by a judge?"

Suddenly, Charlie didn't feel so confident. "Guido lives out in the country by himself. The guns were probably for self-defense."

"That's not what our ballistics expert says. One of the guns is the weapon that was used in the murders of Gretchen Hall and Yuri Makarov."

"I, uh, I didn't see that report."

Fournier handed Charlie a stack of papers. "I just got it. Here's your copy. You might want to ask Mr. Weiss for an explanation," she said, flashing a smug grin.

"You have to get used to calling my client *Guido Sabatini* or he checks out," Charlie said, desperate to change the subject.

"I'll call him by his real name, and I'll ask the judge to hold him in contempt if he causes any trouble about it."

Fournier was definitely angry, and Charlie wondered if that had anything to do with his victory in the drug case.

"So, where did you find Mr. Weiss?" Charlie asked.

"He was selling his paintings in a farmers market in Lincoln City."

Charlie laughed. "I'm not surprised. And doesn't it make you wonder that he wasn't hiding out?"

Bridget flashed an angry smile. "No, Mr. Webb, it does not. I see his actions as those of a person who is trying to manufacture an insanity defense."

Charlie didn't see any point in arguing his case to Fournier. It was obvious that her mind was made up, so he started to walk to the defense table.

"Charlie Webb?" someone called out.

Charlie turned and saw one of the best criminal defense lawyers in Oregon walk through the bar of the court.

Henry Roman was a former United States attorney who had been practicing criminal law on both sides of the aisle for thirty years. He was six feet, two inches tall, 268 pounds, with close-cropped, silver-gray hair and steel-blue eyes that lasered a belligerent stare at any opposing counsel who had the temerity to try to best him. Every day before work, in every kind of weather, Roman rowed for an hour on the Willamette River, and he looked like he could still make the Olympic team he'd rowed on when he was at the University of Washington.

"Yes?" Charlie answered.

Roman held out his hand. "Henry Roman. Judge Noonan appointed me to help out in your murder case."

Charlie couldn't believe his ears. It was as if someone had asked LeBron James to play on his team in a pickup basketball game or Tiger Woods had joined his foursome at his public course.

"That's great," Charlie managed.

"I want to assure you that I'm here as an advisor. You're lead counsel."

"Uh, about that, Mr. Roman—"

"Henry," Roman corrected him with a smile.

"Yeah, well, I'm in way over my head with this case. I told Judge Noonan that I shouldn't be Guido's lawyer. I've never represented anyone in anything more serious than a bar fight, and I'm only here because Guido says he'll represent himself if I'm not his lawyer, which would be a disaster. So, I would be really grateful if you would act as lead counsel."

"Are you sure?"

"Definitely. I think Guido, uh, Mr. Weiss, might be completely innocent, and I'd feel awful if he was convicted because I made a mess of his defense."

"Well, okay, if you're certain I'm not stepping on your toes."

"You have no idea how relieved I am."

"The judge made sure I had a complete set of the discovery in Mr. Weiss's other cases and this one, so I'm up to speed."

"There's other stuff you need to know," Charlie said, and he told Roman about the discovery of the murder weapon in Sabatini's farmhouse, his suspicions that Guido was in possession of something that bore on the sex trafficking case, what had happened at Guido's farm, and the correct way to address their client to avoid a scene.

Bridget Fournier frowned when she saw Henry Roman sit beside Charlie at the defense table. Then she was distracted when the courtroom door opened and Thomas Grant, *the* Multnomah County district attorney, walked down the aisle and entered the bar of the court.

Grant was in his early forties with wavy black hair and an all-star smile. A career politician, he'd won a seat in the Oregon legislature shortly after receiving a master's in political science. Next was a seat in the state senate. Most people in the know saw his victory in the Multnomah County district attorney race as a stepping stone in a bid to be Oregon's governor.

Charlie thought that Bridget Fournier looked surprised and upset when Grant sat next to her. Grant leaned over and whispered something to Bridget. She didn't look pleased.

Two jail guards escorted Guido to the defense table. Guido looked like he didn't have a care in the world, and he beamed at Charlie.

"Mr. Webb, how kind of you to represent me again," Guido said.

"I told you that you made a big mistake by insisting that I be appointed to represent you in your murder case, Guido. Fortunately, Judge Noonan realized that I need help. This is Henry Roman. He's one of the most experienced and successful criminal defense lawyers in Oregon. Judge Noonan appointed him to assist me in your defense, so you're going to have the best representation possible."

Guido turned toward Roman. "Thank you for agreeing to help me. It should help our defense that I am completely innocent."

"You didn't kill Gretchen Hall or Yuri Makarov?" Charlie said.

"I've never killed anyone."

"What happened at your farm? When I came to settle the case, the farmhouse and the barn had been trashed."

"I have an excellent security system. It alerted me to an intrusion by a person dressed like an assassin in a James Bond movie, so I left."

"Did you bring Miss Hall's painting and the other things you took with you?"

"I did, and they are in a safe place."

Charlie wanted to ask some more questions, but Judge Noonan took the bench, and his bailiff called the case. The judge looked surprised to see Grant sitting next to Bridget.

"Welcome to my courtroom, Mr. Grant. Are you representing the State in this case?"

Grant stood. "Miss Fournier is prosecuting the defendant. I'm just appearing with her so the people of our county will know how seriously I take this case."

"Very well. Miss Fournier, are you ready to proceed?"

"I am."

"And Mr. Webb?"

"Uh, Your Honor, I wanted to thank you for appointing Mr. Roman to assist me. I've asked him to be lead counsel because of my inexperience with this type of case."

"Very well."

The bailiff read the indictment, and Judge Noonan asked Guido how he was going to plead. Roman stood.

"Mr. Sabatini will enter a plea of not guilty, Your Honor. And I would like to take up the issue of bail at this time."

Bridget Fournier stood up. "This is a murder case, Your Honor. There is no automatic bail. You'll need to hold a bail hearing so I can put on witnesses to support the State's position that Mr. Weiss should not be granted bail."

"Sabatini," Guido said as he cast a pleasant smile at the deputy DA, who ignored him.

"Normally, that's true," Roman said. "But I've read over the police reports in Miss Hall's and Mr. Makarov's murder cases. Frankly, there is nothing connecting our client to the scene of the crime except his painting. No witness places him there. There is no forensic evidence like a footprint or DNA."

"Mr. Roman has failed to mention that the gun that was used to murder Gretchen Hall and Yuri Makarov was found in Mr. Weiss's farmhouse along with a second gun."

"My cocounsel went to Mr. Sabatini's farm with Miss Hall the day she was murdered. He can testify that Mr. Sabatini was not there and his studio and his house had been searched and ransacked. So, the painting could have been taken at that time, and the murder weapon could have been planted at any time after the murders, because no one was on Mr. Sabatini's property.

"Actually, the painting's presence at the scene, draped across Miss Hall's body, and the gun being found in Mr. Sabatini's house create a reasonable doubt. As I'm certain Your Honor knows, Mr. Sabatini has a genius IQ. Why would someone that intelligent leave evidence like the painting at the crime scene when it points toward him like a neon arrow?

"And Mr. Sabatini would have had to return to his home to leave the gun. Why would he do that instead of getting rid of it? This smells like a setup, Your Honor."

"Miss Fournier, is Mr. Roman correct when he says that there is no physical evidence connecting the defendant to the scene of the murders, except for the painting?" the judge asked.

"And the murder weapon. And you know, because you presided over the arraignment in Mr. Weiss's burglary case, that he stole another painting from Miss Hall's restaurant."

"That fact doesn't bear on whether there is a high probability that Mr. Sabatini committed murder," Roman said.

"I have to agree with Mr. Roman. Miss Fournier, if I held a bail hearing next week, would you be able to produce any other evidence connecting the defendant to the scene where the victims were found?"

"May we have a moment, Your Honor?" Thomas Grant said.

"Of course."

Charlie watched as Fournier and her boss had a heated conversation. Then Bridget addressed the court.

"I can't swear that I could."

"It is unusual to settle the matter of bail at an arraignment for murder," Judge Noonan said, "but given what the parties have told me, I am going to settle the bail question today."

THE JUDGE MET IN CHAMBERS WITH THE LAWYERS AND DECIDED ON AN amount that Charlie's client would have to post to get out of jail. They went back to the courtroom, where the judge put the bail discussion on the record before recessing court.

"Guido, here's my card with the address of my office," Henry Roman said. "When you are released, come over and we'll meet."

"I must go back to my farm to paint. I have lost valuable time away from my studio."

"You'll lose more time if you're sent to death row," Charlie said. "Start taking your case seriously."

"Very well," Guido conceded.

"See you soon," Roman said, and he followed Fournier and Grant, who were just leaving the courtroom with the detectives. Charlie looked at the spectator section, but the blonde was nowhere to be seen.

The guards started to approach Guido to take him back to the jail so he could be processed out, but Charlie held up a hand. When the guards retreated, Charlie leaned close to his client.

"Guido, you are in great danger if you continue to hold on to whatever you took from Gretchen Hall's safe. Hall and Makarov have been murdered, your house and barn were trashed, and I think someone may have searched my office. The people who want what you took from the safe will kill to get it back. Give it to me, and I'll make sure it goes to the DA. If you don't have these things, no one will have a reason to hurt you."

Guido smiled. "I appreciate your concern, but the granting of bail so I can continue to paint is proof that God is protecting me. And I believe he will continue to watch over me as long as I keep these objects in a safe place."

Guido stood up. "Now I must accompany these gentlemen back to the jail so I can be released."

Charlie felt helpless. Then he thought of a way to help Guido.

CHAPTER SEVENTEEN

WHEN CHARLIE WALKED INSIDE THE BUCCANEER TAVERN, HE WAS
greeted by the sound of billiard balls smacking against one another,
raucous hard rock music, and the smell of cigarettes, weed, sweat,
and stale beer. When his eyes adjusted to the dim light, he spotted
Gary Schwartz and Bob Malone drinking at a table with two other
Barbarians.

Gary and Bob had heavy beards, violent tattoos, and massive
builds. Schwartz was very smart, but he had never applied his intel-
ligence in high school. Despite a so-so academic career, his ability
as an offensive lineman had earned him a football scholarship to a
Division II school, where he'd played one year before enlisting in
the marines.

Bob Malone had been a good student in high school, but he'd
had no interest in going to college. He had enlisted in the marines
as soon as he graduated, and he and Gary had been reunited in
Afghanistan. The friends had opened a garage when they returned
stateside, and they were making good money as auto mechanics.

"Hi, fellas," Charlie said, addressing his friends' two companions. "Can I talk to Bob and Gary alone? It's legal business."

All the Barbarians liked Charlie because of his excellent won-lost record in cases involving the club. The two men left the table so Charlie could confer with his friends.

"What's up?" Bob asked.

"I need a favor, and I'll compensate you for your time."

"Speak," Gary said.

Charlie filled them in on Guido's case.

"Now that he's out of jail, I'm certain that someone is going to try to kidnap him so they can find the evidence he took from Hall's safe," Charlie said. "Can you watch his place and protect him until I can figure out how to make him safe?"

"Sounds like fun," Gary said.

"Sounds like shit we did in-country," Bob said.

"Guido is coming to Henry Roman's office as soon as he's released. I'll let you know when we're done, and you can follow him to his farm," Charlie said.

"Consider it done," Bob said.

"Does anything about the bail hearing strike you as weird?" Gary asked Charlie.

"What do you mean?"

"First, there's Henry Roman. He's one of the heaviest hitters in the criminal defense bar. How did you get him as cocounsel? Wouldn't most judges appoint a public defender to help you out?"

"I guess," Charlie conceded. "Judge Noonan must have called in a favor."

"Why? The Constitution guarantees you a competent lawyer. Not a superstar. There must be a lot of public defenders with experience in murder cases. And have you ever heard of bail being granted in a murder case at the defendant's arraignment without a hearing when the murder weapon was found in the defendant's house?"

"I can't answer that," Charlie said. "This is my first murder case."

"It ain't the first one a Barbarian has been a part of." Gary shrugged. "From what you've told us, Sabatini is in danger as long as he is out and about and is hanging on to whatever he took from the safe. Granting bail under unusual circumstances would be something someone would do if they wanted Guido where they could get to him."

"What are you suggesting?" Charlie asked.

"I am suggesting that something smells fishy. What was Thomas Grant doing at an arraignment?"

"The sex trafficking case is super high profile, and Guido is involved in it, someway."

"Still . . ." Gary said.

"You have a suspicious mind, Gary," Bob said. "You're not suggesting that the chief DA for our county has been fucking underage girls, are you?"

"I'm not suggesting anything. I just have a feeling that something ain't right."

Charlie knew that Gary was into conspiracy theories about the deep state, who killed Kennedy, and what one could find at Area 51, so he was desperate to divert him.

"Can I count on you to watch Guido's back?" he asked.

"We're on it," Bob said. "No one will be permitted to fuck with Mr. Sabatini."

Charlie had a drink with his friends before heading downtown. When he was in his car, he thought about what Gary had said. He had read the statutes governing death penalty cases, and he knew that getting bail without a formal hearing was not what normally happened.

And there was something else that was bothering him. Judge Noonan said that he was granting bail because the State hadn't convinced him that their case was very strong. It wasn't. Other than the painting, nothing connected Guido to the scene of the crime or the murders. There was the gun, but anyone could see that it was planted, like the painting, to frame Guido. *So,* he asked himself, *why was the district attorney's office charging Guido? Why hadn't they waited until they had a stronger case?*

One answer occurred to him. Being charged with murder was scary. Did someone want to frighten Guido into letting go of the items he took from Gretchen Hall's safe?

Charlie frowned. Suddenly, he was thinking like Gary, and that wasn't good. He didn't believe in the existence of bigfoot, UFOs, and the Illuminati, and a conspiracy that involved people in power trying to frame Guido to frighten him into turning over the evidence he'd stolen sounded like a crackpot theory. But was it?

CHAPTER EIGHTEEN

HENRY ROMAN'S OFFICE WAS ON THE TWENTIETH FLOOR WITH VIEWS OF the boats cruising the Willamette River, the foothills of the Cascade Range, and the snowy slopes of Mount Saint Helens and Mount Hood. It was a lot different from the dingy suite in the Stone Age office building where Charlie practiced, and Charlie wondered if he would ever have clients whose fees would let him live and work in luxurious surroundings.

Roman had called Charlie as soon as Guido arrived at his office, and Charlie found his client and his cocounsel sipping cappuccinos when he walked into the spacious conference room where they were meeting. Two of Roman's associates were seated at the end of a long conference table that would easily accommodate ten more people.

"Can I get you a cappuccino or a latte?" Roman asked. "One of my associates worked his way through law school as a barista and we have our own coffee bar in the kitchen."

"A caffe latte would be great," Charlie said as he sat down across from Guido.

Roman tilted his head toward the associates, and one of them scurried out of the room and down the hall.

"So, Guido, how are you doing after your jail experience?" Roman asked.

"It was very interesting. Some of my fellow prisoners had interesting physiognomies, which I will incorporate in future drawings."

Roman smiled. "I'm glad the stay was useful. And what will be very useful for you will be an explanation of how your trial will work and how you can help us win it.

"The first thing you have to understand is that a trial where the DA is seeking the death penalty is different from every other kind of criminal trial. There are potentially two trials. One on guilt or innocence, which is like any other trial, and a second trial where the jury decides if you should be sentenced to death if they find you guilty of murder with aggravating circumstances.

"It's this second potential sentencing trial that makes death cases unique. In any other criminal case, there is usually a lot of time between a guilty verdict and sentencing, and the judge decides the sentence. A sentencing hearing in a death case is held immediately after the trial in the guilt phase because the jury that finds you guilty has to decide your sentence. That means that Charlie and I have to assume you'll be convicted—even if we think we can get a not guilty verdict—because we won't have time to prepare for the sentencing hearing if you are convicted. Do you understand the difference?"

"Yes, but I will not be convicted, because I have excellent counsel, I am innocent of the crimes of which I am accused, and God protects me."

"I'm glad you're so confident of the result, but Charlie and I wouldn't be giving you competent assistance if we didn't prepare for all eventualities. One thing we're going to do is prepare your biography starting when you were born and ending at the trial. We need your help to do this. I'll need you to write out your life story with emphasis on any character witness or deed that will convince a juror that you don't deserve to die. Then we'll have investigators collect the evidence we'll use at your sentencing hearing if things go bad. Can you write your bio for us?"

Guido looked uncomfortable. "This will require me to take time from my painting. Besides, all of my mentors in Italia are dead."

Henry Roman looked confused, and Charlie sighed.

"We don't expect to call Leonardo da Vinci as a witness," Charlie said, "but we would like to know about your history in the twentieth and twenty-first centuries. You know, who are your parents, are they still alive, any siblings, your education and friends. Stuff like that."

"This task does not evoke pleasant memories."

"Guido, we need the information if we're going to do a good job defending you."

Guido stood up. "Thank you for your excellent explanation. Now I must return to my farm so I can paint."

"But we have a lot more to discuss," Roman said.

Guido smiled. "I am fatigued from my night in the jail's rough accommodations. We can continue this discussion at another time."

Guido walked out of the room, leaving Roman open-mouthed.

"What was all that about Italy and da Vinci?" he asked Charlie.

"Welcome to my world," Charlie answered with a sigh.

CHAPTER NINETEEN

AFTER TWO NIGHTS OF TROUBLED SLEEP, EXHAUSTION CAUGHT UP WITH Charlie and he slept like a dead person. Good Cup Coffee was near his office building, and he picked up a latte before crossing the street. When he walked into the waiting area, he stopped short so quickly that some of his drink slopped out of the cup.

Sitting on the sofa was the stunningly attractive woman he'd seen in the courtroom when Guido was arraigned on the murder charges. When he'd passed her in the courtroom, Charlie had only seen her face for a few seconds, but he had a vivid memory of short, golden hair, skin the color of porcelain, and eyes of the deepest blue. When the woman stood, Charlie could see that her figure was as amazing as her looks. She was tall; Charlie guessed about five ten. She was wearing tight jeans that showed off her long legs and perfect backside, and a navy-blue blouse that fit just as provocatively and showed off breasts that made erotic fantasies ricochet through Charlie's mind.

"Mr. Webb?" she asked hesitatingly.

"Yes," Charlie answered, struggling to act professionally.

"I apologize for dropping in without an appointment, but I was hoping you could meet with me if you have some free time. I can come back."

"Uh, no. That won't be necessary, Miss . . . ?"

"It's Elin . . . Elin Crane."

"Okay. Why don't you come back to my office. Do you want coffee, tea?"

"No, that's okay."

Charlie told the receptionist to hold his calls. Then he led Crane down a long hall decorated with photos of Mount Hood, Haystack Rock, and other examples of Oregon's scenic beauty.

"So, Miss Crane, how can I help you?" Charlie asked when they were in his office with the door shut.

Elin looked down at her lap. "This is embarrassing."

"I don't judge, Miss Crane, and I've heard it all, so just tell me what's bothering you so I can help."

Elin took a deep breath. "I dated this man just one time. He came on really strong, and I didn't like it. When he asked me out again, I turned him down."

Elin paused and took another breath.

"Do you want some water?" Charlie asked.

Elin looked up and shook her head. Charlie waited for her to gather herself.

"The thing is, he started calling me at all hours, begging me to go out with him again. I was very firm. I said I wasn't attracted to him and he should date someone else. The calls have continued. He leaves voice messages, and I've seen him standing on the sidewalk across from my apartment. He sends me emails. I want it to stop. Can you help me?"

"Yes, Miss Crane, I can," Charlie said. "I can get you a restraining order from a judge. If this man continues to bother you, we can have him arrested. Tell me, was he ever physically abusive?"

"Oh no! After that one date, he was never near me again, except across the street."

Elin was so beautiful that Charlie was having trouble concentrating, so he took out a form he used when he was hired by a new client.

"Before we go any further, there are a few formalities I have to take care of when I have a new client."

"Then you'll take me on?"

"Of course. So, can you spell your full name for me and tell me your address, email, and phone number?"

Charlie didn't know if he would be hired when he told Elin his hourly rate, but he could ask her out if he wasn't representing her now that he had her contact information.

"Do you mind me asking why you decided to hire me?" Charlie asked when Elin told him that his fee would not be a problem.

Elin blushed. "I like lawyer shows on TV, and I'm toying with the idea of going to law school, so I decided to sit in on some cases to see what real lawyers do. Your client, well, it was obvious that he has problems, and I was impressed by how compassionate you were."

Now it was Charlie's turn to blush. "Mr. Sabatini has obvious problems, but I treat every client with dignity."

"I could see that, and that's why I decided to see if you could help me."

"The law is a good profession. I think you'd like it."

"I don't know if I could practice criminal law. Don't you worry when you represent a murderer?"

"Mr. Sabatini's case is my first homicide. And I think he's innocent."

Elin hesitated. "I don't know if I can ask this question, so tell me if it's inappropriate, but I was wondering what Mr. Sabatini did. It sounded like he stole a painting he painted, and now the police think he killed the person who bought it. Is that right?"

"Yes. I can't tell you much about the case, because I can't violate a client's confidence, but he is a very good artist, and he sold a painting to Gretchen Hall, who owns a restaurant. The police are saying that he broke into the restaurant and took back the painting. Then Hall was murdered in Tryon Creek park, and one of Guido's paintings was found at the scene. But he says he didn't kill her."

"If he just took the painting, can you get the charges in the burglary case dropped by returning it?"

"That's what we were hoping to do."

"Was that all he took, just a painting?"

"There may have been something else."

"Oh, what?"

"I really can't say anything more."

"Sorry. I didn't mean to pry. It just seemed like an interesting case."

Charlie didn't want to be rude, but he felt uncomfortable discussing Guido's case, so he changed the subject.

"Do you want me to try and get a restraining order, Miss Crane?"

Elin thought for a minute. "That's a big step. Let me see what he does. Maybe he'll just stop and the restraining order won't be necessary. Can I get back to you?"

"Of course, Miss Crane," Charlie said as he successfully hid his disappointment. "Why don't you let me know, one way or the other."

Elin stood up. "I will. Just talking to you has made me feel a lot better." She smiled. "And you can call me Elin."

Charlie walked Elin to the front of the office and watched her get into the elevator. Then he went back to his office. After fantasizing about Elin Crane for a few minutes, he took a deep breath and turned his thoughts to the task of keeping Guido Sabatini alive.

Charlie thought about what Gary had said after he filled them in on the case. He'd suggested that Thomas Grant might have been involved in the sex trafficking ring.

At Guido's arraignment on the burglary charge, Monica Reyes had told him that she had been given the okay to dismiss Guido's case if he returned everything he'd taken from La Bella Roma. Who had told her? Charlie had another case with Reyes, and he decided to use it as an excuse to find out about Guido's case.

Charlie dialed the DA's office and asked to be connected to Reyes.

"Hi, Monica. Did you get my discovery in Martin Coughlin's DUII case? I wasn't sure I sent it."

"Yeah, it came two days ago."

"Oh, good."

Charlie wasn't sure how to work the conversation around to Guido's case, but Monica saved him the trouble.

"I heard Sabatini has been arrested for killing the owner of La Bella Roma. It looks like we messed up getting him out on recog."

"That wasn't your fault. Didn't you say your boss told you that you could agree to recog?"

"That's true."

"Was that Tom Grant?" Charlie asked.

"Yeah."

"I didn't know he got involved in unimportant cases like Guido's."

"He just dropped by and asked what I had on my table. He was talking with all the lawyers in my unit. So, I hear that Bridget Fournier is livid that Sabatini is out on bail on the murder charge."

"She was upset. But for the record, I don't think Guido is guilty."

"I guess we'll see," Monica said.

"Well, I'm glad you got the discovery. It was good talking to you."

When Charlie hung up, he felt a little sick. Was the chief prosecutor in Multnomah County involved in the sex trafficking ring, or was Charlie getting paranoid? If that were true, who could he call for help in keeping Guido alive? Something Monica Reyes had said gave Charlie an idea.

PART THREE
DESPERATE MEASURES

CHAPTER TWENTY

"WHY ARE YOU CALLING ME?" BRIDGET FOURNIER ASKED.

"I might have some information that will help you prosecute your sex trafficking case," Charlie answered.

"What could you possibly know?" Fournier asked.

"Look, I don't want to be mysterious, but we need to meet in person. And not in your office. You'll see why when we talk."

"Look, Mr. Webb, I'm busy, and I don't have any time for this spy shit."

"I don't know why you're mad at me, Bridget. It's Judge Noonan who granted bail, not me. Please, this is important. A life may be at stake. Can you meet me at the Good Cup coffee shop across from my office? The drinks are on me. I'll even spring for a scone," Charlie said.

There was silence on the line. Charlie waited.

"This had better be good," Bridget said before she disconnected.

CHARLIE WAS SITTING AT A TABLE IN THE BACK CORNER OF GOOD CUP Coffee. When Fournier came in, he waved. Fournier sat opposite

Charlie. She did not look happy. Charlie smiled and pushed a latte and scone across the table.

"As promised," he said.

Fournier didn't look at the scone or the latte. "Let's cut to the chase, Mr. Webb. Why are we meeting?"

Charlie took a deep breath. "Okay, no more small talk. When Guido took the painting from Gretchen Hall's office, he also took some items from her safe. Guido wouldn't tell me what they were, but he seemed certain that Hall would drop the charges in exchange for them. He said he would return the painting and the items from the safe if Hall would agree to hang his painting in La Bella Roma's dining room. Hall agreed to Guido's terms, and we went to his farm to seal the deal. Only Guido wasn't there, and his house and the barn where he paints had been ransacked. Then someone searched my office.

"Do you have any idea what Guido took from the safe? Because I think it's evidence that could be used in your sex trafficking prosecution, and I think Guido is in danger as long as he has the items."

Bridget's features had changed from angry to thoughtful while Charlie was talking. Charlie let her think. After a minute, Bridget looked across the table.

"Your client may be in possession of a snuff film and a list of the men who had sex with the women who Hall procured."

"I was afraid it was something like that." Charlie paused. "You wanted to know why I didn't want to talk about this in the district attorney's office. I had a very good reason. I'm going to say something you might not like. It's just a suspicion, and I hope I'm wrong. It concerns Tom Grant."

Charlie could see he had Fournier's full attention.

"When Guido stole the painting from La Bella Roma, it was

the third time he'd pulled a stunt like that, but Grant told Monica Reyes to agree to his release on recognizance. Then Grant showed up at Guido's arraignment. I could see that you were surprised and upset. I may be crazy, but I'm worried that some powerful people want Guido out of custody so they can find out where he's stashed the items he took from Hall's safe.

"I have two men watching Guido, but he won't pose a threat if you can convince him to give you what he took from the safe. Will you come to his farm and try and convince him to give you what he took?"

CHAPTER TWENTY-ONE

CHARLIE HAD TOLD GUIDO TO EXPECT HIS FRIENDS, SO GUIDO CONTIN-
ued to paint when he heard the growl of two Harleys driving into
the yard in front of the barn. When his bodyguards walked inside,
he put down his paintbrush.

"Hey, Guido. This is Bob, and I'm Gary. Charlie sent us to keep
you safe."

Guido beamed at the Barbarians. "I welcome your assistance,
and, with your permission, I would like to paint your portraits to
show my appreciation."

"That would be nice," Gary said, "but let's table that gesture
until our job is done."

Guido shrugged. "As you wish."

Gary and Bob walked behind Guido and studied his depiction
of a peaceful valley with a waterfall as its centerpiece.

"You're really good, aren't you?" Gary said.

"I had the best teachers."

"Michelangelo and Leonardo da Vinci, right?" Gary said.

Guido smiled.

"We Googled you," Bob said. "You've got a checkered past."

"How so?" Guido asked.

"Don't be shy. We know all about your adventures in the world of gambling. Any tips?"

Guido smiled. "Yes. Don't gamble. I never did when I played poker or blackjack."

Gary smiled, and Bob threw his head back and laughed.

"I'm going to walk the perimeter, and Bob will stay inside," Gary said. "You go back to doing what you're doing and try to forget we're here."

Guido turned to his easel and examined his evolving nature study.

THREE HOURS AFTER CHARLIE MET WITH BRIDGET FOURNIER, TWO OF THE detectives who were working the sex trafficking case drove Bridget to Guido's farm. They followed Charlie into the yard and parked next to him when he stopped in front of the barn.

When Charlie got out of his car, he looked for Gary and Bob. When he didn't see them, he thought they might be in the barn watching Guido paint, but Guido was alone. Bridget and the detectives followed Charlie into the barn.

"Hey, Guido," Charlie said. "How is the painting going?"

Guido frowned. "I am being defeated by the light. Try as I may, I cannot get the correct effect of the sun as it is setting." Guido shrugged. "It is a challenge that I must rise to."

"This is Bridget Fournier. You probably recognize her from the arraignment in your case."

"A pleasure, Miss Fournier. Are you French? I have never painted scenes from France, but I intend to expand my horizons someday."

"My ancestors were from Aix-en-Provence."

"Ah! Have you been there?"

Bridget nodded. "I spent a semester in France during my junior year in college."

"*Bien!*" Guido said with a smile.

"So, Guido," Charlie said, "we're here because we're worried about you. Your farmhouse and your studio were searched, and so was my office. Bridget and I are certain that the people who searched were looking for the items you took from Miss Hall's safe, and we're worried that you're in danger as long as you have these items."

Guido opened his mouth to reply, but he didn't. Instead, he shifted his eyes toward the entrance to the barn. Charlie turned his head and saw three masked men armed with automatic weapons.

Charlie's adrenaline kicked in, and everything moved in slow motion. One of the detectives swiveled toward the front of the barn and drew his gun. Several gunshots echoed through the barn, and the detective staggered and fell. The second detective fired a shot that hit one of the gunmen in the leg before the other two killed him.

Bridget froze. One of the armed men raised his weapon and pointed the barrel at her. Charlie picked up Bridget and dove behind the stack of hay bales on which Guido's paints rested. They hit the ground just as several paint cans exploded, spraying them with a rainbow-colored cloud. The gunman walked toward the bales. Charlie covered Bridget with his body. The gunman looked down at Charlie, and their eyes locked. The killer aimed at Charlie's head.

On a few occasions, Charlie had wondered how he would feel at the moment he died. It was probably the adrenaline working, but now that his death was imminent, he was perfectly calm.

This is it, he thought as he gave himself over to death. Then two explosions rocked the barn. The gunman arched backward, and his weapon flew from his hand. There were several more explosions. Then there was no noise at all.

"You can come out now, Charlie," Gary Schwartz said. "These fuckers are down."

Charlie felt Bridget's breasts pushing into him, and he realized that he was pressed against her. He flushed and rolled off. "Are you okay?" he asked her.

Bridget didn't answer. She seemed dazed. Charlie weighed over two hundred pounds, and he'd fallen on her. He helped Bridget to her feet. She looked down at her clothes. They were spattered with paint, and straw was stuck to her suit in places.

"How you doin', Charlie?" Bob Malone asked. He and Gary were carrying sawed-off shotguns.

"I'm alive, thanks to you two."

"Sorry we were late to the party," Bob said. "We were bored, so we decided to take a beer break when we saw you and your friends drive up. We're allergic to cops, so we made ourselves scarce until we heard the gunshots."

Charlie stared at the carnage. The man who was going to shoot Charlie and Bridget was sprawled on the barn floor. Part of his head had disappeared. A second killer had a gaping wound in his chest. The third hit man had been shot by one of the detectives. He was alive, but his breathing was ragged.

Charlie bent over and threw up. Bridget helped him sit on a hay bale and gave him a handkerchief he used to wipe his mouth.

"Sorry," he apologized.

"Don't be. I'd be dead if you hadn't tossed me over the hay bales." Bridget took out her phone.

"Who are you calling?" Charlie asked.

"We need an ambulance, a crew from the crime lab, and homicide detectives."

Charlie looked alarmed. "What about my friends? I don't want them to get in trouble."

"Didn't you tell me that you hired them to protect Mr. Sabatini?"

"Yes."

"Then they did their jobs, and they saved our lives too. No one is going to come after them."

"Gary will see to your man until the ambulance arrives," Bob said. "He was a medic in the marines."

Bridget started making calls, and Charlie noticed Guido. He had a wide smile on his face, and he was working on his painting.

"What the fuck, Guido? Were you just standing there while everyone was shooting?"

Guido shrugged. "God protects me."

"Are you an idiot? You could have been killed."

"Not while I have the items from the safe. No one shot at me."

"That's because they wanted you alive so they could torture you to force you to tell them where you hid the stuff you took from the safe. If you give the items to Miss Fournier, no one will have a reason to hurt you, and you can paint in peace."

Bridget turned toward Guido. "Mr. Sabatini, do you have a list with the names of men who had sex with women at Leon Golden's estate and a film of one of these girls being murdered?" she asked.

"Maybe."

"That's evidence that can put evil men behind bars. Don't you think God would want you to help me punish these men for what they did?"

"The ways of the Lord are mysterious. I don't know why he has saved me, but I believe it is because I have kept the items from the safe."

Charlie could see that Bridget was getting frustrated.

"You know I can have you locked up for obstructing my investigation?" she said.

"Do what you think is right," Guido said.

"That's not going to work, Bridget," Charlie said. "Guido will sit in your jail cell until hell freezes over."

Bridget sighed. "You're right." She turned to Guido. "At least let me put you somewhere where you'll be safe."

"I am perfectly safe here."

"Will you be okay with my leaving people to protect you?"

Guido shrugged. "Do as you wish. As long as they do not interfere with my painting, I don't care."

Bridget shook her head. Then she went over to the wounded detective and stayed with him. When she heard sirens, she walked into the yard. Two ambulances followed by a marked and an unmarked police car stopped in front of her. Charlie watched her talk to the officers, detectives, and medics. A minute later, the medics carried the wounded detective and gunman to different ambulances.

Bridget walked over to Bob and Gary. "One of the officers was upset about the sawed-offs. I told him you two saved my life and no one could touch you. But they do need your statements. Would you be willing to tell one of the detectives what happened? I was on my back, staring at the ceiling, and I have no idea."

"No problem," Gary said.

Bridget led the two Barbarians over to a man who was standing next to the unmarked car and introduced them. Then she walked back to Charlie.

"I told the lead detective what I knew. I also said that we were really shaken up. He's going to let us give a full statement tomorrow. Is that okay with you?"

"You bet."

"I came with the detectives, so I don't have a way to get back to town. Could you give me a lift?"

"Definitely."

Bridget looked embarrassed. "In all the excitement, I never thanked you for saving my life. You were very brave."

Charlie turned red. "Brave is when you know what's going on, you weigh your options, and do the right thing. Honestly, Bridget, I can't even remember what I did. I just reacted."

Bridget smiled. "Don't get all modest on me, Charlie. A coward would have saved himself. I'd be dead if it weren't for you."

Charlie's flush deepened.

"Hey," Bridget said, "I don't know about you, but I'm starving. Do you think that's a normal reaction after what we went through?"

Charlie smiled. "I don't know what you've been through in your life, but this is my first time being attacked by homicidal assassins, so I can't answer your question. But I could go for a stack of pancakes."

CHAPTER TWENTY-TWO

CHARLIE DROVE TO A RESTAURANT THAT SERVED BREAKFAST ALL DAY. Bridget was quiet during the ride, and Charlie didn't feel much like talking either. When they parked, Bridget got out and looked down at her paint-spattered clothes.

"God, I look like a piece of abstract art."

Charlie laughed and took off his suit jacket. "Put this on and only the bottom of your skirt will show."

"Sir Walter Raleigh would be proud of you," she said as she slipped on the jacket.

Charlie and Bridget ordered pancakes, bacon, and coffee.

"The people behind the attack at the farm must be desperate if they're willing to attack a DA and police detectives," Charlie said when the waitress left with their order.

"What Guido has must be dynamite," Bridget agreed. "Do you have any idea how we can convince him to turn it over?"

Charlie shook his head. "The guy's a space cadet."

"Or a really cool customer. He was right, you know. Those hit men never took a shot at him."

"Something just occurred to me," Charlie said. "Those killers showing up at his farm just when we did. Was that a coincidence, or did they know you were coming?"

"How would they know?"

"Did you tell anyone we were meeting at the coffee shop?"

"I mentioned it to Nick DeCastro, the head of the unit, because you said you had info about our sex trafficking case. And one of the detectives could have said something."

The waitress brought their coffee, and Charlie and Bridget stopped talking. While the waitress set out their napkins, forks, spoons, and knives, Bridget thought about the attack. It was an act of desperation, and that gave her an idea.

"Did you grow up in Oregon?" Charlie asked when the waitress left, anxious to talk about anything that would create distance from the terrible events in the barn.

"No, Chicago," Bridget answered.

"How did you get out here?"

"I applied to law schools on the West Coast, and Lewis & Clark offered me a scholarship. What about you?"

"I'm a third-generation Oregonian. Did you always want to be a prosecutor?"

"Oh yes. My folks owned a grocery store in a dangerous area— lots of drugs, lots of guns, lots of wrecked lives. They were robbed so many times that they sold it. I was old enough to understand how awful that decision had been for them, and I've wanted to put bad guys away since I was a little girl."

Charlie smiled. "You seem to be living your dream. None of the defense attorneys I know want to lock horns with you."

Bridget laughed. "You didn't do so badly."

Charlie blushed. "I got lucky."

"You destroyed my arresting officer. That had nothing to do with luck."

Charlie's blush deepened. "He shouldn't have lied."

"Too true. I was really pissed. He lied to me from the get-go, and we had a long talk after the case ended."

"Oh, I thought you were mad at me because the judge granted my motion."

"I'm sorry you thought that. I was never mad at you."

Before Charlie could say that he was glad, the waitress brought their order, and they both dug in, grateful that the act of eating kept the horror of the shoot-out at bay.

CHARLIE DROPPED BRIDGET AT HER CONDO IN SOUTHEAST PORTLAND and drove home. As soon as he was in his apartment, he stripped off his dirty clothes and headed for the shower. While the hot water pounded down on him, he smiled as he thought about their meal at the restaurant. Bridget had put away a stack of pancakes smothered in maple syrup, and four strips of bacon. Most of the women he dated asked if their food was gluten-free, wouldn't touch a slice of bacon with a ten-foot pole, and barely touched what the waiter brought because they were watching their figure.

Before their ordeal, Charlie had a pretty negative opinion of the prosecutor. He'd seen her the way most of the defense bar did—a rigid, hard-nosed DA who lacked a sense of humor. He still didn't think she'd cut him a break, despite what they'd gone through together, but she seemed less like a killing machine now that he'd spent some time with her. And he was definitely relieved that her anger in Peter Easley's case was aimed at her witness and not at him.

Charlie toweled off and dressed in sweats. Then he got a beer and sat on his sofa and channel surfed, looking for a show that would help him forget his near-death experience.

BRIDGET FOURNIER'S CONDO WAS CLOSE ENOUGH TO THE WILLAMETTE River and high enough to give her a view of Portland's skyline, but she had no interest in the view when she was safely inside.

She took off her paint-stained clothes and dropped them on the floor. Then she walked into her shower. When the hot water poured down on her, she began to shake. She sank down on the floor of the shower and let the water cascade over her as she recalled how close she'd come to dying. If Charlie Webb hadn't thrown her over the hay bales, she would not exist.

She took deep breaths to calm herself. She was alive. She was not dead. She had survived. She was okay. Thanks to Charlie Webb.

The only other contact she'd had with Charlie had been in the Peter Easley case. Everyone in the office had assured her that he wasn't too bright and wouldn't put up much of a fight. But they'd been wrong. Charlie had surprised her by figuring out that her key witness was lying, then proving it in court. Today, he had fooled her again by saving her life when most people in their situation would have saved themselves.

Bridget stopped shaking. She stood up, grabbed the soap, then the shampoo, and scrubbed the horror off her skin and out of her hair. When she was completely clean, she threw on sweats and clean socks. Then she poured a stiff shot of very good scotch she saved for special occasions, having decided that not dying constituted a valid reason for celebrating.

While she sipped her drink, Bridget thought about Charlie. To date, she had not had a successful romantic relationship. There had been close calls—a romance in law school with a boy who couldn't handle the fact that Bridget was smarter than he was, and a brief fling with a partner in a civil firm. Nothing had stuck.

Bridget liked how humble Charlie had been after saving her life. And if memory served, he hadn't gloated after beating her in court.

She took another sip of scotch and decided to stop thinking about Charlie Webb. They were on opposite sides of a murder case, and that ruled out any chance of getting to know him better. Assuming that he would want to know her better.

After a while, she focused on an idea she'd gotten while they were eating their pancakes. It wasn't a great idea, but it might have great results if it worked. She would flesh it out tomorrow. Today, she was going to find the dumbest comedy movie on her television and try to forget the sight of the gun barrel that had come within inches of her face.

CHAPTER TWENTY-THREE

CHARLIE SPENT THE EARLY PART OF THE NEXT DAY AT POLICE HEADQUAR-ters telling a homicide detective everything he could remember about the shoot-out at Guido's farm. When he finished, he went to his office.

Elin Crane was sitting on a couch in the reception area. Before he could go to her, his receptionist stood up and stared.

"Are you okay?" she asked. "It was all over the TV and the internet that someone tried to kill you."

"I'm fine," Charlie said as several of the lawyers, secretaries, and paralegals in the suite crowded around him and wouldn't drift off until he assured them that he was in one piece.

Charlie started to talk to Elin, but the receptionist interrupted him.

"Mr. Webb, Mr. Roman called several times. He wanted you to call him as soon as you got in. He said it's urgent."

Elin stood up. "Do you have a moment to meet with me?"

"I do, but I have to make a call first. Can you wait?"

"I can come back."

"No, wait. This won't take long."

Charlie shut his office door. He was sure he knew why his co-counsel was calling. He'd acted impulsively when he'd met with Bridget Fournier and asked the DA to come to Sabatini's farm. It had dawned on him when he was home and safe that he should have called Roman before talking to Bridget.

"The shoot-out is all over the news. Are you okay?" Roman said when they were connected.

"Miraculously, yes."

"They said that you went to Guido's farm with Fournier."

"That's right."

"So, the reporters got it right? You took the person in charge of sending our client to death row to talk to him?"

"Uh, well, I had an idea."

"A fucking bad, awful idea. What were you thinking, and why didn't you run it by me? That's what cocounsels are for. We're supposed to tell you that the idea you thought was so brilliant is really, really stupid."

"You're right. I went off half-cocked."

"What were you trying to do?"

"I thought Bridget could convince Guido to turn over the evidence he took from Hall's safe, and we could make a deal."

"Jesus, Charlie. Did you think Fournier would let Guido walk?"

Charlie felt awful. "I guess I didn't think it through. I was more worried about getting Guido out of danger."

"And how did that work out?"

"I fucked up, okay? From now on, I won't do anything without talking it over with you. I promise."

Charlie heard Roman take a deep breath.

"What's done is done," Roman said. "I'm glad you're alive. Meanwhile, I have my associates working up a jury questionnaire and working on some legal issues that might come up. We'll meet soon."

Charlie ended the call. He felt like a fool. What had he been thinking? It was becoming crystal clear that he had no business being within a thousand miles of a death penalty murder case.

Suddenly, Charlie remembered that Elin Crane was waiting to see him. He buzzed his receptionist and told her to show Elin to his office.

"I wanted to tell you that my problems with the stalker seem to be over," Elin said when she was seated across from Charlie. "I haven't seen or heard from him since we met, so it looks like I won't need the restraining order."

"That's great," Charlie said, trying to sound enthusiastic even though this meant that Elin wasn't going to be a client.

Elin hesitated. Charlie thought she looked nervous.

"Actually, there's another reason I came in today," she said. "I heard about what happened at that farm, and I wanted to see if you were okay."

"Thanks for asking. I was shaken up, but I wasn't hurt."

"Is Mr. Sabatini okay?"

Charlie laughed. "While the bullets were flying, and everyone was ducking for cover, he kept painting." He shook his head. "Guido is completely insane."

"Why is someone trying to kill him?"

"I can't get into details, but Guido came into possession of some things that are a threat to some very powerful people."

"Does this have something to do with the sex trafficking case?"

"What makes you think that?"

Elin shrugged. "Mr. Sabatini is accused of killing two of the people who were charged in that case."

"The items might have some relevance to that case, but I really can't say anything more."

"I'm sorry. I shouldn't be so nosy."

"That's okay."

"Mr. Sabatini's case is your first murder trial, isn't it?" Elin asked.

"Yeah."

"Is it hard, defending someone who could go to prison for the rest of his life?"

"I'm not enjoying myself. Quite frankly, it's more responsibility than I want, but I have to do it because I don't think Guido killed anyone."

"It must help to have someone like Henry Roman on your team."

"Most definitely. I really don't have the experience to try the case on my own."

Elin paused. She looked uncomfortable. "I had another reason I wanted to see you today."

"Oh?"

"I had a really weird idea. I was a journalism major, and I'm really good at research, and I was thinking that I might be able to help you with Mr. Sabatini's case."

Charlie looked alarmed. "You're not a reporter, are you?"

"Oh, no. I'm not doing a story, and I'd never stab you in the back by getting information from you and selling it to a paper."

Charlie flushed. "I'm sorry. I didn't mean to accuse you of anything."

"No apology necessary. I can see where learning I was a journalism major could freak you out."

It suddenly dawned on Charlie that he would be able to see Elin every day if he accepted her offer of help.

"I couldn't pay you," he said.

"Oh, I wasn't thinking of getting paid. I told you that I was thinking of going to law school, but I wasn't sure that's what I wanted to do. Working on a murder case would give me real insight into what it would be like to be a lawyer. That's why I want to help you."

"Well, okay. Let's try it out," Charlie said, thrilled that he would have an excuse to be with Elin. "I think there's a small office that no one is using. I'll ask the managing partner if you can work there."

Elin flashed a wide smile. "Thank you, Mr. Webb. I really appreciate you letting me do this."

Charlie returned the smile. "If we're working together, it's Charlie."

Elin left, and Charlie ran through his voice messages. He deleted most of them because they were from reporters. He was almost through his emails when his receptionist told him that Guido Sabatini was in the waiting room.

Charlie didn't want to deal with his client, but he couldn't send him away. He sighed and told the receptionist to send Guido back. Moments later, Guido walked into Charlie's office holding a small painting in front of him.

"What are you doing here? Where are your guards?"

"Two nice policemen escorted me here. They are in the waiting room."

"Didn't they tell you to stay on the farm?"

"Of course, but they checked with their superiors and were told that I had a constitutional right to confer with you."

Charlie sighed. "What is that?" he asked, pointing at the painting.

"Your office is so drab that I want to brighten it up with this sunny view of Venezia."

Guido walked to an empty space above Charlie's bookcase and held up a colorful view of the Grand Canal. Charlie thought it was beautiful, and there was no question that his office was pretty boring.

"Thanks, Guido. I appreciate the gift."

Guido had brought nails, hooks, and a hammer. When he finished hanging the painting, he beamed.

"It looks great," Charlie said. "But it's hanging in my office, where no one else can see it. Am I safe?"

Guido laughed. "I promise I will not liberate it."

Charlie smiled. "So, I won't have to ramp up my security?"

"Not on account of me, Mr. Webb. And now I must return to my studio. I'm glad you weren't hurt."

As soon as the door shut behind Guido, Charlie walked over to the painting. Guido had gotten the light just right. Charlie sighed. Guido was a pain in the ass, but he was one hell of an artist, and his gift had lifted Charlie's spirits.

Then he remembered that he would be seeing Elin Crane every day. Yesterday had been the worst day of Charlie's life, but today was turning out okay.

CHAPTER TWENTY-FOUR

THE MORNING AFTER THE INCIDENT AT GUIDO SABATINI'S FARM, BRIDGET
Fournier gave a detailed statement to Gordon Rawls. She was almost finished when Sally Blaisedale walked into the interview room.

"How are you doing?" the detective asked.

"Not great. But I'm coping."

"We've had some developments I wanted to tell you about."

"Oh?"

"None of the shooters had any ID on them, so we searched the woods surrounding Sabatini's farm looking for anything that would help us identify them."

"Did you find out who they are?"

"Yes, but we also found a dead man in the woods. He had been shot, and he'd been there for a while. He had ID in his wallet. His name is Brent Atkins."

"Do you have any idea why he was at Guido's farm?"

"We've talked to his brother, Brad. He said he and his brother play in a backroom poker game in Clackamas County. Sabatini sat in and cleaned them out. They found out that he was a brilliant poker player who used to play in high-stakes games in major casinos. Brad said that his brother is a hothead and went to Sabatini's farm to beat him up."

"Do you think that Sabatini killed him?"

"We tested the two guns that were found during the search of Sabatini's farm. Atkins was killed with the same gun that was used to kill Gretchen Hall and Yuri Makarov."

"What about the shooters? Do you know who they are?"

"Yes. The shooter who was taken to the hospital died last night, and we never got a chance to talk to him, but we matched their fingerprints to military records. They were all Navy SEALs, but they went private four years ago with an outfit called National Security, which is owned by a man named Max Unger.

"And there's one more thing we learned. I showed photos of the three shooters to Sabatini. He recognized one of the dead men. He visited the farm and called himself Rene LaTour. LaTour said he was a San Francisco art dealer who was representing a wealthy client who wanted to buy several of Sabatini's paintings. After they'd talked about the paintings, LaTour offered a large sum of money for an item that had been removed from Gretchen Hall's safe. Sabatini said he cut off the discussion when it became clear that LaTour had no interest in his art."

"Did he tell you what the item is?"

"He clammed up when I asked him. But it's pretty damn clear that some very dangerous people want it."

THE HEADQUARTERS OF NATIONAL SECURITY WAS IN A TWO-STORY BUILDING surrounded by Quonset huts, a shooting range, and a makeshift town where the employees could practice raids, hostage situations, and other scenarios that they might have to encounter.

The headquarters building was painted dull brown, and the entrance was guarded by serious men toting automatic weapons. Blaisedale, Rawls, and Fournier flashed their credentials. After a short wait, they were shown into Max Unger's second-floor office.

Unger was a little under six feet tall, but he had the squat, thick physique of an NFL fullback. He wore khaki pants and a navy-blue, short-sleeve shirt that showed off his corded, tattooed biceps and forearms. Unger's nose had been broken and poorly reset, he wore his gray-black hair in a buzz cut, and a cauliflower ear on the right side of his head was evidence that he had an acquaintance with combat sports.

The office of the president of National Security was strictly utilitarian. There were no granite-topped tables or floor-to-ceiling windows. Just a large, scarred wooden desk, metal filing cabinets, two client chairs, and a whiteboard that hung on one wall.

"Thanks for seeing us on such short notice," Bridget said.

"On the phone, Detective Blaisedale said that three of my employees murdered a detective and tried to assassinate several other people. That definitely got my attention."

Gordon Rawls opened a file folder on Unger's desk and spread out photographs of the three dead shooters.

"Are these the men who were at the farm?" Unger asked.

Rawls nodded. "Do any of them look familiar?" he asked.

Unger studied the pictures. Then he shook his head.

"In the States, National employs men and women with military and police experience for security details for CEOs, celebrities, and politicians. But we also send men into war zones to supplement America's armed forces and assist other nations' militaries. Because

I'm the head of the company, my work is mostly administrative. I'm not involved in hiring or training our employees, who, over the years, have numbered in the thousands. So, no, I don't recognize these men, but you can talk to my head of HR.

"There is one thing I can say for certain. If these men attacked a police officer or prosecutor, they weren't acting as employees of National Security. Men like these are mercenaries who parlay their military training into lucrative contracts far in excess of what they are paid by the US military. It wouldn't surprise me if they were hired by someone who is not connected to my company and who ordered the hit."

Rawls looked at Fournier and Blaisedale, who indicated that they didn't have anything more to discuss with Unger.

"I would like to look at the employment files for these men," Bridget said.

"I'll clear that for you. HR is on the first floor. Sorry I couldn't be of more help."

When they were in the hall and headed down to HR, Rawls turned to Bridget and Blaisedale.

"What do you think?" he asked.

"I don't know," Bridget said. "Unger sounded sincere, but . . ." She shook her head. "We need to see if there's any way to tie any of the shooters to Unger before we can move on him."

CHAPTER TWENTY-FIVE

ELIN WAS WAITING FOR CHARLIE WHEN HE WALKED INTO THE RECEPTION area at nine thirty.

"When did you get here?" Charlie asked.

"When the office opened at eight."

Charlie's cheeks turned red with embarrassment. "Come on back," he said as he led Elin down the hall to his office. He waited until she was seated across from him.

"I'm impressed by your initiative, but I don't have that many cases going now, and I tend to get in late. Let's agree that I'll call you when I need you. I cleared it with the managing partner, so you'll have your own office. If you have a project, come in when you want to. Otherwise, let's coordinate."

Now it was Elin's turn to look embarrassed. "Sorry. I didn't know when you'd want me, so I thought I should be here."

"No need to apologize. I appreciate the initiative. I should have set some ground rules."

Elin thought she should change the subject, so she pointed at Guido's painting. "That's new, isn't it?"

Charlie turned toward the painting, then back to Elin. "It's a gift from Guido."

"I sure hope we can clear his name, because he's one hell of a painter."

Charlie's cell rang. It was Bridget Fournier.

"I have to take this," he said.

Elin started to stand, but Charlie waved her down. Charlie had the speaker function on, and Elin heard Bridget ask Charlie how he was doing.

"I slept okay last night. How about you?"

"I'm back to work. That's why I called. I learned some interesting information about the men who attacked us."

"Oh?"

Bridget filled Charlie in about the killers' employment history with National Security and Rene LaTour's visit to Sabatini's farm.

"Whoever sent LaTour to Charlie's place also sent the assassins who tried to kill us," Charlie said.

"That's obvious."

"Do you think Unger is responsible for murdering Hall and Makarov?" Charlie asked.

"I don't want to discuss our case. I just thought you should know what I found out about the men who tried to kill us."

"You're right. I shouldn't have said anything about Guido's charges. Thanks for sharing. I appreciate it."

Bridget ended the call, and Charlie sat back and tried to digest the information Bridget had given him.

Elin looked excited. "You think the men who tried to kill you also murdered Hall and Makarov, don't you?"

"I think it's possible. I have to call Henry Roman to tell him what I just learned. We might want to argue that the killers at the barn also murdered Hall and Makarov to raise a reasonable doubt at Guido's trial."

"That could work," Elin said.

"Thanks for coming in, Elin. I don't have anything for you to work on right now, but I'll try to get some work for you to do, and I'll call you when I've figured out something that won't waste your time."

Elin left, and Charlie called Roman.

"So, you think we have a viable suspect to give the jury if we want to raise a reasonable doubt about our client being the only person with a motive to kill Hall and Makarov?" Roman asked.

"Don't you?"

"This is good ammunition, Charlie. Let me put my investigators on Unger and see what they turn up."

Charlie felt his chest swell when the call ended because he'd made a positive contribution to Guido's defense.

CHARLIE HADN'T SPOKEN TO BOB OR GARY SINCE THE SHOOT-OUT, AND he felt bad that he hadn't checked in with them, so he drove to their garage instead of heading home. He found them working on a German sports car. He held out an envelope stuffed with cash.

"I come bearing gifts."

Gary wiped his hands on a rag before opening the envelope and counting the cash Charlie had stuffed inside.

"I figured you'd prefer cash to a check," Charlie said with a smile.

"What Uncle Sam don't know can't hurt him," Gary said.

"How did the cops treat you?" Charlie asked.

"One guy was an asshole because of the sawed-offs, but that nice DA lady straightened him out," Gary said. "Everyone else was real appreciative after she explained that she and the other detective wouldn't be alive if we hadn't come to the rescue."

"Count me in that group," Charlie said.

"We only saved your ass because you hadn't paid us yet," Bob said.

"That's why I didn't pay you up front," Charlie answered with a smile.

"Fucking lawyers," Gary said.

"Seriously, I do owe you my life, and so do several other people."

"Hey, we aim to serve and protect," Gary said.

"Booyah!" Bob added.

"How do you feel about continuing in that vein?" Charlie asked.

"You want us back on guard duty?" Gary asked.

"I thought the cops had that covered," Bob said.

"They have two officers watching Guido, but the men who attacked us had military training."

Charlie filled in his friends on what he'd learned about Max Unger and National Security. "I'd feel a lot better about Guido's future if you two were watching his back."

"This sounds like it's above our pay grade," Bob said. "We only had to deal with three men. Next time, there could be a whole platoon."

"I'm not asking you to die to protect Guido. If the next group that comes after him is too big to handle, bail."

"Let us think on it, Charlie," Bob said.

"Deal. And thanks again for what you did."

"For a guy who almost died, you sound pretty chipper," Gary said.

Charlie blushed. Gary looked at Bob.

"It's got to be a chick," Bob said.

"Fuck you," Charlie said.

His friends started laughing.

"Spill," said Bob.

Charlie realized that it would feel good to talk to his friends about Elin. "Okay," he admitted. "There's this woman. She came to see me about a restraining order."

"Did you restrain her?" Gary asked.

"You're an asshole, Gary," Charlie said.

His friends cracked up again. Charlie gave them the finger and started to leave.

"Wait," Gary said. "I'm sorry. We'll be serious. I promise."

Charlie hesitated.

"Come on," Bob said. "You know we always have your back. So, this is serious, this woman?"

"No. It's nothing like that. She's just really good-looking and really nice. And she volunteered to work on Guido's case to help me out."

"For nothing?" Gary asked.

"She's thinking of going to law school, and she thought that seeing how a murder case is tried might help her decide."

"And you like her?" Bob asked.

"I think so. Yeah."

Gary clapped Charlie on the back. "Well, good luck, then. And if you need any advice on how to get the fairer sex in the sack, I'm your man."

"Jesus, Gary, you are the last person I'd ask for relationship advice."

"Too true," Bob said. "All the women he fucks leave in the morning after they sober up."

"And on that note, I think I'll end this conversation," Charlie said. But he had a big smile on his face during his ride home.

CHAPTER TWENTY-SIX

WHEN BRIDGET HAD BEEN EATING PANCAKES WITH CHARLIE, SHE HAD decided that the attack on her and the detectives had been an act of desperation, and that had given her an idea. When she got back to her office, she called Morris West, Leon Golden's attorney, and said that she wanted to meet with West and his client at her office to discuss a deal. An hour later, West returned Bridget's call. He said that Golden would listen to what she had to say, but after Makarov's and Hall's murders and the incident at the farm, he didn't feel safe leaving his estate.

At four that afternoon, Sally Blaisedale and Bridget stopped at the main gate and told a security guard their names. A few minutes later, the prosecutor and the detective got their first view of Leon Golden's mansion. Men with dogs were patrolling the estate, and Bridget's gut tightened when she saw the logo on their jackets.

"Golden's guards work for National Security," Blaisedale said.

"I noticed."

Bridget parked in a turnaround in front of the house, and two armed guards walked to her car. Bridget and Blaisedale flashed their identification.

"I apologize," one of the security guards said, "but in light of everything that's gone on, I have to make sure you aren't armed."

Bridget and Blaisedale could have refused to disarm, but confronting Golden was more important than forcing a showdown, so they surrendered their sidearms and submitted to a pat-down. When the guards were satisfied, they escorted Bridget and Blaisedale through a marble-tiled entryway, past a curved stairway that led to an upper floor, and down a hall to a study where Morris West and his client waited.

West was in his early sixties and dressed in a navy-blue, hand-tailored suit, a blue Hermès tie that matched the color of his suit, and a cream-colored silk shirt. His bald head had a fringe of gray hair, and he had grown a mustache and goatee to compensate for the hair loss. Bridget had dealt with West before, and she knew from experience that the Harvard grad was always at the top of his game.

West radiated confidence, but his client looked uncomfortable. Golden was wearing gray slacks, a blue shirt, and a gray sweater. His tan had faded because he had not gone outside of his mansion since his release on bail, and the styled hair he'd sported on the red carpet looked faded and loosely combed.

"Good afternoon, Bridget," West said. "We heard about your ordeal at the farm. Are you okay?"

"Thanks for asking, but I'm fine."

"We appreciate your driving out," West said. "With everything that's happened, I assume you of all people can appreciate why Leon wanted to meet here."

Bridget smiled at West's client. "You have a beautiful estate, Mr. Golden. It's too bad you have to hole up here. But I have a proposition for you that might allow you to feel more secure."

"We're listening," West said.

"I think that Mr. Weiss has a list of the men who had sex with the girls you supplied and a copy of a snuff film that was shown to the girls to frighten them into having sex. The people who sent the men who attacked me at the farm and murdered Gretchen Hall and Yuri Makarov must be desperate to get them back, and there's a good chance that you are their next target because you can give me the names of the men on the list. If you cooperate, I can offer you a lesser sentence and protection."

Golden flashed a humorless smile. "If I cooperate with you, no one can protect me."

"That may be true, Mr. Golden, because you are employing guards from National Security, the firm that employed the men who tried to kill me at the farm."

The color drained from Golden's face.

"Is that true?" West asked to cover his surprise.

"Max Unger claims that the men were no longer working for his firm, but they were employed by National Security at one time. I've seen their employment records."

"Was . . . was Max Unger . . . Did he send them?" Golden blurted out.

"Don't say anything else, Leon," West warned his client.

"Is Mr. Golden acquainted with Max Unger, aside from hiring his guards from his firm?" Bridget asked.

Golden looked at his attorney, who shook his head.

Bridget shrugged. "If Unger is one of the men on Weiss's list, employing his firm to protect your client is like inviting the fox into the henhouse."

"I think Mr. Golden and I have a lot to discuss," West said. "We will consider your offer, and we'll get back to you."

"You know where to find me, Morris. Oh, by the way, Mr. Golden, are you certain that no one has planted any listening devices in your house? You might want to hire someone who doesn't work for National Security to check it out."

Bridget left the mansion and drove back to Portland with a smile on her face.

AS SOON AS BRIDGET AND BLAISEDALE LEFT, GOLDEN BEGAN TO PACE. He was sweating, and he looked distraught.

"Do you know someone who can check the house for wiretaps?" Golden asked his lawyer.

"I do know someone, but I don't think it's necessary."

"Well, I do, and I want the house swept ASAP."

"Fournier was playing mind games with you. No one has been tapping your phones or bugging your rooms. You've got to calm down, Leon."

"Don't tell me to calm down. Just get someone out here who can find out if my house is bugged."

"All right. I'll call when I get back to my office."

They talked for fifteen more minutes before West drove back to town. As soon as he was alone, Golden grabbed a burner phone and called Max Unger.

"Why are you calling me?" Max Unger asked.

"Did you send the men to Weiss's farm?" Golden asked.

"You're asking me a question like that on a telephone?"

"It's a burner, and I'm asking because the prosecutor in my case and a detective just left my house after telling me that the men at the farm worked for you, and they think your men murdered Gretchen and Yuri."

"They visited me too, and I told them that the men who shot up the farm did work for National Security, but they weren't employed by us now. And no one I know killed Yuri or Gretchen."

"But the men from the farm did work for you?"

"I never heard of them until the detectives told me, Leon. I employ hundreds of men and women all over the world, but I only know a handful personally."

"Am I in danger?"

"From me? Of course not. I have my people protecting you because someone killed Yuri and Gretchen."

"I don't know what to believe."

"You've got to hold it together, Leon. The only reason you'd be in danger is if you made a deal with the DA."

"Is that a threat?"

"I'd never come after you, but there are a number of powerful people who might if they thought you were going to name names. As long as you don't cave and cooperate with the authorities, you're safe."

"Okay. I get that," Golden said, but his mouth was dry and his heart rate was through the ceiling.

"One more thing," Unger said. "Do not call me again."

BRIDGET WAS IN HER OFFICE FOR LESS THAN A HALF HOUR WHEN Thomas Grant walked in.

"Hey, Bridget," Grant said as he took a chair across from his deputy. "I hear you were out at Leon Golden's estate."

"Who told you?"

"Morris West. He said you threatened his client."

"That's absolutely false. I'm certain Gretchen Hall and Yuri Makarov were murdered because of their involvement in Golden's sex trafficking ring. I told him that he was in danger too, and we could protect him if we made a deal. I did want to scare him, but I did that by laying out facts, not threats."

"I guess Morris put a spin on the visit," Grant said.

Bridget looked directly at her boss. "Yes, he did."

"Is Golden going to make a deal?"

"Morris was going to let me know tomorrow, but I take his whining to you as an indication that he's not."

"Where does our case stand?" Grant asked. "We're getting close to the trial date."

"I was certain that I could turn Gretchen Hall. Now that she's dead, the case is floundering. The women will testify, but they have no evidence to support their claims."

"So, we're in trouble?"

"There is one possibility. When Lawrence Weiss stole a painting from Hall's restaurant, he also took something from her safe. He won't say what it is, but the attack on the two detectives and me is strong proof that the people involved in the sex ring are desperate to get it back. If I can get Weiss to give me what he has, it might give us a winning hand."

"But you don't know what he has?"

"No."

"And he won't turn it over?"

Bridget sighed. "Weiss is insane, but Charlie Webb, his lawyer, is desperate to convince Weiss to give me what he has. He knows

Weiss's life is in danger as long as he holds on to the evidence from the safe."

"It sounds like the success of our case hinges on Webb's ability to convince his client to make a deal," Grant said.

Bridget sighed. "I'm afraid you're right."

CHAPTER TWENTY-SEVEN

CHARLIE'S EUPHORIC FEELING ONLY LASTED UNTIL ELIN CRANE CALLED two hours later.

"What's up?" Charlie asked.

"I found out something you're not going to like."

Charlie looked at his watch. "Why don't you tell me over lunch?"

"We need a place where we won't be overheard," Elin said. She sounded nervous.

Charlie named a bar a few blocks from his office, and Elin walked in shortly after he arrived.

"What did you find?" Charlie asked after the waiter left with their order of burgers and beers.

"I ran an internet search looking for connections between Roman, Grant, Hall, Makarov, Golden, and Unger, all of the people involved in some way in Guido's case." Elin paused. "Henry Roman represented Max Unger in a civil case three years ago."

"Unger is Henry's client?"

"He was. I haven't found any other case where he represented him since then."

"Henry didn't tell me."

"There's more. With the exception of Makarov, everyone I named is a member of the Westmont Country Club."

"That makes sense. It's Portland's most exclusive club. Hall, Golden, Roman, Grant, and Unger are wealthy or prominent members of Portland society."

"If Roman represented Unger, it's logical to assume that they interacted at the Westmont, but Roman didn't tell you about the connection," Elin said.

"Maybe he didn't think it was important," Charlie said. "You said it was a three-year-old case."

"Is he still a client if the case is over?" Elin asked.

"I'm not sure. I mean, he would be for the old case, but . . . I don't know."

"You should ask him."

"I will. And you did good work."

Elin beamed. "Thanks, Mr. Webb."

"Charlie," he corrected. "And I appreciate your initiative."

"Thanks."

Charlie would have stayed with Elin all day, but he had to ask his cocounsel why he hadn't told him that Max Unger was a client. So, he reluctantly ended their meeting and headed back to his office.

"I'm glad you called," Roman said as soon as he answered Charlie's call. "I was going to call you. We have a problem. Guido isn't writing his bio, and he refuses to discuss his life story with the associate I sent to his farm. Can you talk to him? You seem to be able to get through to him."

Charlie sighed. "I'll try, but he's tough to move once he gets his mind set on something. Uh, there was a reason I wanted to talk to you. Remember I told you that the men who tried to kill me worked for Max Unger at National Security?"

"Yes."

"Uh, well, I just found out that you represented Unger in a civil suit three years ago."

"I did?"

"Yeah. Do you think that's a problem?"

"Okay, I remember now. The case involved his accountant, who was claiming he'd been fired because of discrimination. I didn't handle the case. One of my associates did. The matter was over very quickly, and I haven't seen or talked to Unger since I closed the case."

"Not even at the Westmont? I've been told that you're both members."

"What's up, Charlie? This sounds a lot like a cross-examination."

Charlie was embarrassed about bringing up the relationship, but he knew he couldn't let the matter drop.

"No, it's not like that. I'm just worried that you might have a conflict if we try to argue that someone connected to Max Unger murdered Hall and Makarov."

"I don't see any problem."

"Should I check with the ethics counsel at the bar to see what he thinks?"

"Sure, if you want to. But I don't think I have a conflict."

"Yeah. Okay. But I thought I should ask you."

"I'm glad you did, Charlie. Like I said before, we need to work as a team."

Charlie felt much better when the call ended. He decided that he could call the bar later, and he'd just thought of a way that might get Guido writing his bio.

PART FOUR

THE LIFE OF THE ARTIST AS A YOUNG MAN

CHAPTER TWENTY-EIGHT

CHARLIE DROVE INTO GUIDO'S BARNYARD, AND ELIN FOLLOWED CLOSE behind in her car. A police officer walked over to Charlie's car. Charlie lowered his window and showed the officer his bar card.

"I'm Guido's lawyer." Charlie pointed toward Elin, who was getting out of her car. "That's my assistant, Elin Crane."

"That's okay, Mr. Webb. I recognize you."

"Is my client in the barn?"

The officer nodded. "He's painting away. My partner is watching him."

"Have you had any trouble?"

The officer shook his head. "It's been real peaceful."

"I hope it stays that way," Charlie said as he got out of the car and headed for the barn, with Elin close behind.

A second officer stood up when Charlie and Elin walked into the barn. Guido stopped painting.

"It's okay, Rhonda," the first officer said. "This is Mr. Sabatini's lawyer."

"Mr. Webb, to what do I owe the honor of this visit?" Guido asked.

"I wanted to introduce you to the latest addition to your defense team, Elin Crane."

Guido started to smile. Then he frowned. Seconds later, he was smiling again.

"I am charmed, Signorina Crane." Guido turned to Charlie. "Why have you brought this lovely woman here?"

"She's going to help you write your biography so we can prepare for the penalty phase of your trial, if that becomes necessary."

"Ah, but it will not, because you are going to win my case at trial."

"We've been over this before, Guido. Henry and I would be judged incompetent if we didn't assume the worst and prepare for a penalty phase. Elin won't interfere with your painting. She'll interview you while you paint."

Elin beamed an irresistible smile at the artist. "I love your work, and I'm excited to see you create a painting from scratch. I promise I'll try to not be a distraction."

Guido hesitated. He studied Elin, and the frown returned. Then he shrugged.

"Very well. You have an interesting face. Perhaps I will put you in one of my paintings."

"That would be an honor," Elin said.

"I'll leave you two," Charlie said. "See you back at the office, Elin."

Charlie left. Elin seated herself on a hay bale and took a legal pad out of a book bag she'd carried into the barn. She thought Guido might resent being recorded.

"What are you working on?" Elin asked.

"A street scene in Siena. Have you ever been there?"

Elin nodded. "I spent a month in Italy and France. I liked Siena, but I loved Florence and Venice."

"Ah, Venezia. My heart is always there."

"It must be, given how many of your paintings are set there. Tell me, did you travel while you were in college or grad school?"

"Both."

"Is that when you started painting?"

"I have always painted, but mathematics distracted me."

"It sounds like you had a great career as a mathematician. Why did you stop?"

Guido lowered his paintbrush and stared at the wall of the barn, lost in thought.

"The numbers were too much for me," he answered, his voice barely above a whisper. "They went on and on. String theory, multiple dimensions, infinity. It was overwhelming. They never ended. I needed something that would stay still. My paintings are frozen in time. They bring me peace."

"What did your parents think when you gave up your academic career?"

Guido's features darkened. "I do not want to discuss my parents."

"You didn't get along?"

"Miss Crane, please do not persist in this line of questioning."

"Okay. I didn't mean to upset you. Can we talk about your career as a gambler? It sounds like you were very good."

Guido smiled. "That is true. I was able to compete with some excellent players of poker."

"Did your proficiency at mathematics help?"

"Of course. But a firm grasp of psychology is even more important."

"Why did you stop?"

Guido laughed. "It became too hazardous to continue. Dangerous people resented the fact that I was smarter than they were, and I received threats. Sometimes these people tried to take action, but"—and here Guido smiled—"I was prepared."

"I've read that you were a consistent winner at blackjack."

"That is true. I have a great ability to count the cards in the game of blackjack. This ability does not please the people who own the casinos, so they banned me." Guido shrugged. "As I said, the playing of cards became too dangerous, so I stopped."

"You seem to have good instincts for avoiding danger. Doesn't holding on to the items you took from Miss Hall's safe put you in danger?"

"Everyone seems to think so."

"Don't you worry that there will be more attempts on your life? You'll be safe if you turn over what you took to the district attorney. Mr. Webb seems to think he might be able to make a deal with the DA so you won't have to go to trial if you give the prosecutor what you took."

"That is what many people say."

"I can see how important painting is to you. Your trial could last weeks, even months. You won't be able to paint very much while your case is being tried. Doesn't it make sense to turn over the items from the safe?"

Guido closed his eyes and took a deep breath. "I am tired. I will go into my house and take a nap. Thank you for visiting me."

Guido's refusal to discuss turning over the items from the safe was frustrating.

"When do you want to continue?" Elin asked when it became obvious that Guido was done talking to her.

"I will let Mr. Webb know when I am ready," Guido said as he cleaned his paintbrush. "Now I must sleep to regain my strength."

Guido walked out of the barn, and the officers followed him into his house. Elin watched them go, her lips drawn in a tight line.

CHAPTER TWENTY-NINE

CHARLIE RETURNED TO HIS OFFICE AND WORKED ON A DIVORCE FOR A woman his aunt had referred. He had just finished talking to the husband's lawyer when his receptionist told him that he had a call.

"Who is it?" Charlie asked.

"She says that she's Mr. Weiss's mother."

Charlie sat up in his chair. "Put her through."

"This is Charlie Webb," he said when they were connected.

"Are you my son's attorney?"

"I'm representing Lawrence Weiss. Are you his mother?"

"Yes. How . . . how is he?"

"He seems to be doing okay."

"It said on the TV that he thinks he's a painter who studied with Michelangelo."

"That's true."

Charlie heard a sob on the other end of the phone.

"My poor boy," she said. "He had so much promise."

"Mrs. . . . Is it Mrs. Weiss?"

"It's Adler. Miriam Adler. I took my maiden name back when I divorced Larry's father."

"I'm so glad you called. We've been trying to get as much background on Larry as we can. Are you still in touch with Larry's father? I need to talk to everyone who knew him when he was growing up."

"Jerry passed away four years ago."

"I'm sorry."

"I'm not. His father drove Larry away."

"Tell me what happened."

"Larry is big now, but he was small and sickly as a child. My husband wouldn't hide his disappointment. And I think he was jealous because Larry was so much smarter than we were. So, he made Larry's life hell until Larry grew. But when he was little, Larry retreated into a fantasy world. I think that's why he pretends to be someone he isn't now."

"This is all very important. Do you live in Oregon? Can we get together?"

"I live in Massachusetts. That's where Larry grew up. He ran away the day after he graduated from high school. I haven't seen him since then, but I read that he went to a college in California." She sighed. "It makes sense that he would want to get as far away from us as he could."

"Have you been in contact with Larry since high school?"

"No. And I'm not surprised he never tried to get in touch. Larry had a growth spurt in high school, and he built himself up so he was very strong. The day he graduated, Jerry got on him. When Larry talked back, Jerry tried to hit him."

Charlie heard another sob. "Are you okay?"

"It's very hard for me to think about that day."

"What happened?"

"Larry defended himself. He beat Jerry so bad that he had to go to the hospital. That's why Larry ran, although he might have been planning to escape for a while. He was always thinking ahead."

"Did your husband tell the police?"

"No. He was too embarrassed, and I threatened to leave him if he did. Then, when it became clear that Larry was gone for good, I ended the marriage." Charlie heard a sigh. "If I'd left Jerry sooner, maybe things would have been different. Maybe I could have protected my boy."

"Ms. Adler, do you want to come to Oregon for Larry's trial? I can send you a ticket and put you up in a hotel."

"No. I can't come unless Larry says that he wants to see me. I don't think he does, and I don't want to upset him."

"Can I send someone to Massachusetts to interview you? If Larry is convicted, your testimony might save his life when the jury is deciding his sentence."

"I have to think."

"Okay. You have my number. Can you tell me how to get in touch with you?"

Ms. Adler hesitated. Then she gave Charlie her contact information. As soon as the call ended, Charlie leaned back in his chair. He felt as if a weight had been lifted from his shoulders. Ms. Adler had helped him understand his client's erratic behavior and had provided valuable information he could use to humanize Guido if he faced a death sentence.

Shortly after Charlie ended the call with Guido's mother, Elin walked into his office. She didn't look happy.

"How did it go?" Charlie asked.

"Not great. Guido cut me off as soon as I asked about his early life. Then he claimed he was tired and went into his house."

"Don't feel bad. That's just Guido acting weird, which is what he does best."

Elin was holding a memo. She gave it to Charlie.

"These are my notes of our conversation. He did open up about why he stopped studying mathematics, but there's not anything else that we didn't know already."

"The stuff about the numbers is interesting," Charlie said when he finished reading Elin's notes, "but not getting him to talk about his early years might not matter. His mom called me."

Elin sat up. "She did?"

"I have a lot of new information we can use if there's a penalty phase."

Charlie briefed Elin on his conversation with Miriam Adler.

"She's a gold mine," Elin said when Charlie was through.

"That she is." Charlie looked at his watch. "Hey, it's lunchtime. Are you hungry?"

"Now that you mention it, I am."

"Do you like Middle Eastern food?"

"It's one of my favorites."

"I'll call Henry. Then I'll take you to my favorite Middle Eastern restaurant," Charlie said.

"That sounds great."

Charlie dialed Henry Roman's number.

"What's up, Charlie?" Roman asked, and Charlie told him about his conversation with Guido's mother.

"That's a real breakthrough," Roman said. "What are you going to do with the information?"

"I'm going to visit Guido to see if I can use what I've learned to get inside his head."

"Good luck with that," Roman said.

"I'll give it the old college try."

"If anyone can get through to Sabatini, it'll be you. And while we're talking, I have something to tell you. Judge Noonan is hearing our pretrial motions, but I can't be in court with you."

"Why not?"

"I've got to go to San Francisco to try and settle a case."

"Maybe we should ask for a set over. I don't feel comfortable representing Guido by myself."

"Hey, Charlie, there's nothing complicated about these motions. A first-year law student could handle the hearing. We've discussed the issues, and we know how the judge is going to rule."

"You're right," Charlie admitted. "Go to Frisco. I'll be fine."

"I wouldn't go if I didn't think you understood the legal issues."

HABIBI WAS A FEW BLOCKS FROM CHARLIE'S OFFICE. THEY ENTERED THE restaurant and sat near the front window. Charlie couldn't believe how much time he was spending with Elin. This made their second lunch in as many days. He wondered what she would say if he asked her to go to a movie or dinner, but he was afraid to ask because he still couldn't convince himself that someone as beautiful and smart as Elin could ever want to have a serious relationship with him. Plus, he'd read enough newspaper stories about romances between employees and supervisors that had gone sour to know that a workplace romance could end very badly.

"So, Charlie," Elin asked after the waiter took their orders, "did you always want to be a lawyer?"

"Honestly, I didn't have any idea what I wanted to be. I have great parents, but my dad works in a factory and my mom is a clerk in a department store. Neither one went to college, so I didn't have any guidance about what to do after high school. And my grades were never that good. I liked lawyer shows on TV, so that's why I applied to law school after college, but I was rejected at almost every law school I applied to. I was lucky one school took me."

"None of that matters now, though, does it?" Elin said. "You've ended up where you would have even if you went to Harvard. You're a practicing member of the bar and cocounsel in a high-profile murder case with national coverage."

Charlie smiled. "It does sound like I'm doing okay when you put it that way."

"You're a good lawyer, Charlie, and you're going to clear Guido's name. I just know it."

Charlie laughed. "Thanks for the vote of confidence."

He had never thought of himself as anything special as a lawyer, but now that he thought about it, a lot of his clients had said the same thing after he'd helped them, and so had Bridget Fournier.

As soon as Charlie paid for lunch, he told Elin that she could go home. Instead of going to his office, he walked to his garage. His talk with Guido's mother had given him an insight into Guido's behavior that he had not had before, and he had decided that a trip to Sabatini's farm might prove useful.

CHAPTER THIRTY

HENRY ROMAN MADE THE CALL ON A BURNER PHONE AS SOON AS THE call with Charlie ended.

"We may have a big problem," Roman told the man on the other end of the line.

"Calm down and talk to me."

Roman related what Charlie had told him. "He's going to use the information the mother gave him to get Sabatini to turn over the flash drive. You know what that means."

"Of course I do."

"We've got to stop him."

"'We'? Are you going to take care of the problem?"

"You mean . . . No. I couldn't . . ."

"I didn't think so."

"Can you get Max to try again?"

"He'll be reluctant after what happened the last time he sent his men after Sabatini, but he'll have to. He's the only one trained for this kind of thing."

"He's got to do it soon. Webb is going to the farm to talk to Sabatini."

"There's the motion hearing. Sabatini will be vulnerable going to court and returning to the farm."

"Great idea. I won't be at the hearing."

"Oh. Where do you plan to be?"

"I told Webb I was going to San Francisco, but I could go anywhere that's not near Portland when this thing goes down."

LEON GOLDEN CALLED MORRIS WEST IN A PANIC.

"You were wrong, Morris. I'm being spied on. The man you sent went over the whole house. There are taps on my phone and microphones secreted around the house."

"You're kidding."

"Do I sound like this is funny?"

"Did Lucas have an idea who installed the taps?"

"No, but he said it was the type of devices the military uses, and who do we know who runs a private militia?"

"You think Max Unger is listening in on your conversations?"

"I don't know, but his men are all over the estate, day and night. They could have done it while I was sleeping. What should I do, Morris? Is Max going to kill me? Do you think he killed Gretchen and Yuri?"

"That crazy painter has been charged with killing Yuri and Gretchen," Morris said.

"What if he was set up? What should I do? If Max's men are going to murder me—"

"You'd be dead by now. If Max killed Yuri and Gretchen, he'd have come after you too. Look, I'll talk to Lucas and see if he has any idea who put the listening devices in your house. Meanwhile, try to get a hold of yourself. I don't want someone calling me and telling me that you're in the hospital with a coronary."

West ended the call, and Golden stared at the phone. He shut his eyes and took deep breaths. That didn't help, so he went to his bar and took out a bottle of single-malt scotch.

OREGON IS THE NINTH-LARGEST STATE IN THE UNITED STATES, BUT ITS population is only slightly more than four million people, most of whom reside in Portland, Eugene, Salem, and Medford, cities that are located on I-5, the interstate highway that runs from Mexico to Canada. Once you are a relatively short distance east or west of the highway, you find small towns and wilderness.

Max Unger waited until the sun went down before driving toward the coast. Suburban developments yielded to farmland before all signs of civilization disappeared on either side of a two-lane highway that ran between evergreen forests.

After he'd been driving for three-quarters of an hour, Unger spotted the break in the towering trees and turned off the highway onto an old logging road. A quarter of a mile in, he saw a car with its lights off parked on the side of the road. Unger stopped next to the car, and the drivers rolled down their windows.

"Two days from now, there's a hearing on pretrial motions at ten in the morning," the man in the first car said. "They'll bring Weiss to court. That's your chance to grab him when he returns to the farm."

"You have to find someone else," Unger said. "A DA and some detectives came to National Security. They know men who worked for the firm attacked the farm, and Webb knows Henry represented me in a case. I can't be involved anymore."

"You don't get it, Max. You are involved, whether you like it or not. If the authorities get their hands on the flash drive, we're all going to prison. Once they see the movie, you'll be an accessory to murder."

"I'm already an accessory to murder. A second attempt on Weiss is too big a risk."

"You don't have a choice. No one else has the personnel to pull this off. Weiss is under tremendous pressure to turn over the flash drive. He's only holding on to the drive because he's crazy. If he were sane, he'd have given it up a long time ago. Webb could convince him to turn over the drive at any moment."

"He's got police guarding him around the clock."

"And you can muster overwhelming force. You do this kind of thing all over the world for two-bit dictators. This time, you'll be doing it to save your life."

CHAPTER THIRTY-ONE

CHARLIE DROVE INTO THE BARNYARD AT A LITTLE AFTER THREE. THE PO-lice officer who came out of the barn told him that Guido was working on a painting. Sabatini turned from his easel when Charlie walked into the barn.

Charlie said, "Hey, Guido. How's it going?"

"*Molto bene!*" Guido answered with a wide smile.

Charlie guessed that meant that Guido thought he was doing just fine.

"Can you take a break and go for a walk? It's nice out, and I wanted to have a talk about something important that just came up."

Charlie walked into the sunlight, and Guido followed a minute later. They walked around the barn and into the field behind it. One of the police officers followed at a discreet distance.

It had rained earlier in the day, and the grass and the air smelled fresh and clean. Neither man spoke for a while, enjoying the hot sun and the clear, blue sky. After a while, Charlie broke the silence.

"I'm a pretty lucky guy, Guido. I was no superstar as a kid, but my folks were there for me while I was growing up. We're close. I see them when I can."

Charlie noticed that Guido was suddenly tense.

"I mention this because I know it's not that way in a lot of families." He stopped and turned toward his client. "I know it wasn't that way in your family."

"I am finding this conversation uncomfortable," Guido said as he turned back toward the barn.

"I knew you would, but don't run away. Let's talk."

"I do not want to talk about my family."

"I know that, and I know why. Your mother saw you on TV, and she called me."

Guido froze.

"She told me about the way your father treated you. Your mother divorced him as soon as you left, and he passed a few years ago, so he can't hurt either of you anymore. She loves you, Guido, and I could tell that she regrets not protecting you when you were little."

"Too little, too late," Guido said, his voice barely above a whisper.

"I don't blame you for thinking that, but you're an adult now, not a weak child. When you were small, were you able to defend yourself when your father beat you? I only talked to your mother on the phone. I didn't see her. Was she strong enough and big enough to fight off your father when he was drunk and in a rage, or was she as weak as an adult as you were as a child? You can't blame yourself for not fighting back when you were small, and you can't blame your mother for not protecting you if she wasn't strong enough to do it."

Guido turned toward Charlie. He looked furious, and Charlie suddenly realized how big and powerful Guido was.

"I could have killed him. I should have killed him for what he did to me. And she never said a word. She ran away when he . . ."

Guido stopped. His shoulders sagged, and his anger drained away.

Charlie reached out and laid a hand on his client's shoulder. "She was powerless, just as you were powerless until you grew big enough and strong enough to defend yourself. She couldn't grow, so she was always powerless, until you destroyed your father and set her free. Can you see that?"

Tears ran down Guido's cheeks, and his chin fell to his chest.

"This is a lot to handle, so let's stop now," Charlie said. He handed Guido an envelope. "Your mother's phone number and email address are in here. Think about what I said. Think about whether you can forgive your mother. If you can, think about whether you want to talk to her. I'll respect the decision you make."

Guido didn't answer, and he looked lost as he headed back.

"Are you going to paint?" Charlie asked.

"No, I have no heart for painting right now," Guido answered. "I think I will rest for a while."

Guido sounded so sad it broke Charlie's heart. He said goodbye when they reached the front door to the farmhouse. When Charlie left, he felt awful. He also hoped that he'd done the right thing and that Guido would start taking his case and his future seriously.

PART FIVE
THE TRIALS OF SAINT SABATINI

CHAPTER THIRTY-TWO

BRIDGET FOURNIER AND SALLY BLAISEDALE SPOTTED CHARLIE AT THE table farthest from the door as soon as they walked into Good Cup Coffee.

"Thanks for coming," Charlie said. Bridget thought he sounded nervous.

"We shouldn't be having these meetings," Bridget said.

"I know," Charlie answered. "Henry was furious when I took you to see Guido without telling him."

"I assume you didn't tell him you were meeting me."

"No. Did you tell Grant?"

"No."

"Neither one of us knows who we can trust. Henry didn't tell me that Max Unger was a client, Thomas Grant made sure that Guido isn't in custody, and who knows who else is trying to get back whatever Guido took from the safe?"

"After what happened at the farm, you don't have to sell me," Bridget said. "So, why are we having this secret meeting?"

"I think that the men who are after Guido are desperate by now. They know that Guido is unpredictable and could turn over the item at any time. Judge Noonan is hearing pretrial motions in Guido's case. That means that Guido is going to be traveling to court and back to the farm. If there's going to be another attempt to kidnap him, it's going to be on the day of the hearing."

"That makes sense," Sally said.

"What do you want us to do?" Bridget asked.

CHAPTER THIRTY-THREE

CHARLIE WOKE UP WITH A NERVOUS STOMACH ON THE DAY JUDGE Noonan had set to hear pretrial motions in Guido's case. Not only was he anticipating an attack on his client, but Henry Roman was trying to settle a case in San Francisco, and Charlie would be on his own.

He knew that the hearing wouldn't last long and the issues weren't that complicated, but his gut was still in knots because he was afraid that he would make a mistake that would hurt his client. He was also very nervous about being the center of attention in a case that was being covered by all the major national news networks.

While he showered and shaved, he remembered that Bridget thought he was a good lawyer, Judge Noonan said he tried a good case, and most of his clients had nice things to say about the way he handled their cases. It didn't help, and he was a wreck by the time he left his apartment.

He had asked Bridget to have the police who were guarding

Guido drive to the apartment so he could arrive at the courthouse with his client. An unmarked car was parked out front. Just before he got in the back seat, Charlie spotted two Harleys parked a block away.

He had convinced Guido to trade his caftan for a suit when he went to the hearing on the pretrial motions, but he was still shocked to see how professional his client looked. Guido had trimmed his beard and cut his hair, and he was wearing a charcoal-gray pin-striped suit, a cream-colored shirt, and a conservative blue tie with white and red stripes.

"You look great," Charlie said. "Everyone is going to think you're the lawyer and I'm the client."

Guido smiled. "I have been reading books about the law. Being an attorney doesn't seem so hard."

"Well, there you are. When you've put this case behind you, you can go to law school."

"I think not. It would interfere with my painting."

Charlie was tempted to ask Guido if he'd tried to contact his mother, but he didn't want to upset his client, and he figured Guido would tell him if he'd talked to her.

Guido's bodyguards parked in a space designated for police cars and escorted Charlie and Guido to the corridor outside the courtroom. Charlie grabbed his client by the arm and steered him through the mob of reporters, answering the questions hurled at them with a repeated "No comment."

Once they were safely inside the courtroom, Charlie led Guido toward the bar of the court. He noticed Gary and Bob sitting in the back of the spectator section. As he walked down the aisle, Elin flashed him a warm smile. Charlie had asked her to take notes, and she was sitting near the front of the spectator section.

Bridget and Thomas Grant occupied the prosecution table. Charlie nodded at them before taking his seat.

"How long will it be before I can go home and paint?" Guido asked.

"The hearing shouldn't be long," Charlie said just as the judge took his seat on the bench.

"Good morning," Anthony Noonan said. "Are the parties ready to proceed?"

Thomas Grant stood. Charlie was certain that Grant knew little or nothing about the issues that would be discussed and that Bridget had written the legal memos in support of the State's positions, but this way, Grant would get his name in the news stories as the lead prosecutor.

"The State is ready, Your Honor," Grant said.

"Mr. Sabatini is ready, Your Honor," Charlie said.

Charlie had filed motions to have the death penalty declared unconstitutional. He wasn't surprised when the judge denied them. His arguments had been litigated at the state and federal levels and had not prevailed, but he had to make a record for an appeal in case Guido was sentenced to death.

"Let's move to your motion in limine, Mr. Webb. I'm going to exclude any mention of the thefts from the steak house and the other Italian restaurant, but I'm going to allow the prosecution to introduce evidence that Mr. Sabatini sold a painting to Miss Hall, then broke into her restaurant and took it and other items."

Charlie and Henry Roman had concluded that Judge Noonan would rule the way he had and that they didn't have any strong arguments for excluding the evidence about the theft from La Bella Roma.

"I have nothing to add to the arguments Mr. Sabatini made in the memo in support of our motion, and I object to your ruling with regard to allowing the State to introduce evidence about the sale and liberation of the painting and the other objects from La Bella Roma," Charlie said.

Judge Noonan smiled. "You've made your record, Mr. Webb. Does the prosecution have a problem with my ruling?"

"We object to the exclusion of the evidence about Mr. Weiss's course of conduct," Grant said.

"Okay. Anything else? If not, I'd like Mr. Webb, Miss Fournier, and Mr. Grant to come into chambers so we can go over scheduling."

Everyone stood when Judge Noonan left the bench.

Charlie, Bridget, and Thomas Grant spent half an hour in Judge Noonan's chambers working out the details of jury selection and the trial. Charlie wouldn't have minded chatting with Bridget, but she was with her boss, and he decided it would make her look bad if Grant felt that they were too chummy.

Charlie told Guido the schedule Judge Noonan had set for the trial.

"Why don't you head back to your farm," he said. "And remember the words *No comment* when we get ambushed in the hall by the members of the Fourth Estate."

Guido smiled. "I will follow your instructions to the letter."

Gary and Bob intercepted Charlie just inside the courtroom.

"Is the blonde who was sitting behind you the woman you've got the hots for?" Gary asked.

Charlie blushed.

"I completely get it," Bob said. "Good luck."

CHAPTER THIRTY-FOUR

GUIDO HATED WEARING A SUIT, BUT CHARLIE HAD INSISTED. HE'D FOUND the suit, the shirt, and the tie he'd worn to court in the back of one of his closets, a relic of his days in academia. As soon as he was in the back of the car heading toward his farm, Guido stripped off his jacket, took off his tie, and unbuttoned the top button of his dress shirt. Now that he was down to shirtsleeves, he felt he could breathe again.

He was anxious to get back to the farm so he could finish a painting of the Ponte Vecchio in Florence. He smiled. Being on trial for murder had turned out to have a silver lining. The online sales of his artworks had skyrocketed, and there had been feelers from several art galleries about showing his work. Guido guessed that the old adage was true: there was no such thing as bad publicity.

He leaned his head back and shut his eyes, assuming that the trip would be as uneventful as all the other trips he'd taken to and from the courthouse. His bodyguards assumed the same thing. That's why they didn't notice the black van that merged onto the highway after they had traveled four miles.

Guido opened his eyes when the car left the two-lane highway and turned onto the bumpy, unpaved road that led to his barnyard. His bodyguards parked in front of the farmhouse. The moment they got out of the car, two armed men in ski masks ran from the side of the house, wrenched open the passenger's and driver's doors, and pointed guns at the officers.

"Don't resist and we won't kill you," the man on the driver's side said.

When the officers got out of the car, they were thrown on the ground, and their hands and ankles were secured with plastic ties. Another armed and masked man walked out of the house and onto the porch just as the black van that had been following the unmarked car raced into the yard. Guido looked at the van through the rear window. Four more masked men got out. Seconds later, he was pulled out of the car and his hands were secured with plastic ties. Two men waited outside to watch the police officers. Another man marched Guido into his living room and threw him onto a chair. Three more men took up positions in the house. Then the man on the porch followed Guido into the living room and stood over him. Guido smiled.

"That was dramatic. I hope the two officers aren't injured," he said.

"You should be worrying about yourself, Larry."

"I am Guido Sabatini."

Max Unger smashed a gloved fist into Guido's nose. Guido squeezed his eyes shut as pain laced through him.

"You are who I say you are, Larry. You'd better stow the Renaissance painter bullshit and get into the real world if you want to survive."

"This is about the flash drive, is it not?"

"Very good."

Guido shrugged. "I am no longer in possession of the drive."

"Where is it?"

Blood ran out of Guido's nose, but he still managed a smile. "That is for me to know and you to find out."

Unger hit Guido again. "No jokes, asshole. Those punches were an amuse-bouche. Several of my men are experts at extracting information. Keep fucking around and I'll turn you over to them."

"In my day, they used the iron maiden and the rack. They caused unbearable pain, and their victims would say anything to stop it, resulting in many false confessions. Torture me and I will send you here and there looking for the flash drive in places where you will not find it."

"We're way past iron maidens and the rack, Larry. We use pharmaceuticals that can get the most stubborn man to tell us what we want to know. Sadly, some of them cause permanent brain damage."

"Do what you must," Guido said.

Unger sighed. "I was hoping this would be over quickly. Unfortunately for you, I'm going to take you somewhere I can extract the information I need without worrying about being interrupted."

Unger turned to two men who were standing in the living room doorway. "Get this idiot to the compound."

The men pulled Guido to his feet. When they were outside, Guido frowned. His bodyguards and the men watching them were nowhere in sight. His captors were just as puzzled, and they stopped on the porch and looked around.

AFTER CHARLIE'S MEETING WITH BRIDGET FOURNIER AND SALLY Blaisedale, Sally had talked to Gordon Rawls, and they'd cashed in a raft of favors to assemble the team that was watching Guido's farm. They had moved into position in the woods that surrounded the farm hours before Guido had been driven to court in case an attempt to kidnap Guido was made in the morning.

Bridget hadn't told Thomas Grant or anyone else in her office about the surveillance because she wasn't sure who she could trust, and she was monitoring the activity at the farm in Charlie's office.

Sally Blaisedale had called Bridget shortly after Guido and his bodyguards left for court to report that a car had parked on the side of Guido's house, where it wouldn't be seen when Guido returned to the farm. Three armed men had gotten out. None of them were wearing masks, and one of the men was Max Unger. Bridget felt like she'd won the lottery.

Charlie had argued that Bob Malone and Gary Schwartz should follow the unmarked car that was taking Guido to and from the farm because no one would mistake them for cops and they were definitely not involved in the sex trafficking ring. His argument had won over Bridget and Blaisedale, and the Barbarians followed Guido from the courthouse on their Harleys, careful to stay far enough back so they didn't spook anyone who was tailing the unmarked car with evil intent. Four miles from the courthouse, their strategy paid off, and Bob phoned Sally Blaisedale.

"A black van just pulled in behind Guido's car," Malone told Blaisedale.

"You're certain it's following Guido?"

"Pretty sure. It settled in a few car lengths back and hasn't taken any of the exits. Here's the number of the license plate."

"Good work, Bob," Sally said before phoning Bridget and telling her the license number of the black van.

Just as the car that was transporting Guido parked in front of the farmhouse, Bridget called Sally.

"The van is registered to National Security," the prosecutor said.

"Bingo," Sally answered.

"Once Unger is in custody facing kidnapping charges, he'll cut a deal and tell us everything he knows about Golden's sex trafficking ring."

"From your lips to God's ears," Sally answered moments before two armed men ran up to the unmarked police car.

"Gotta go," Sally said, ending the call as Guido's bodyguards were pulled out of the car and Guido was hustled into the house. Snipers had the green light to shoot the men who had grabbed Guido's bodyguards if they looked like they were going to harm them.

When Guido was inside, the rescue team moved down from the woods. Several members of the team edged along the side of the farmhouse. The captured police officers were lying on the ground next to the car. The men watching them looked bored. One man was leaning against the unmarked car, his back to the farmhouse. The other man was on his phone. Neither man looked alert, and neither man had his hand on his gun.

As soon as the man who was on his phone turned his back to the house, Rawls raced to him, looped an arm around his neck, and brought him to the ground. The man struggled for a few moments and then lost consciousness.

The other guard heard the sounds of the struggle. When he turned, he found several guns aimed at him.

"Make one sound and I will shoot you," Sally Blaisedale told him.

The officers and the two masked men were hustled out of sight. A few minutes after the men had disappeared, two men dragged Guido out of the house. They stopped on the steps that led to the porch and scanned the yard. The unmarked police car was present, but the captured officers and their guards were absent.

"Where are Frank, Harold, and the cops?" one of the men said.

"I don't know," the other man said. He turned in a circle, scanning the barnyard in an effort to solve the mystery, and found himself facing several men who were pointing weapons at him.

Guido smiled. "The cavalry has arrived."

"Shut your mouth, asshole," Guido's captor said as he pulled Guido in front of him to use as a shield. He pressed the barrel of his gun to Guido's temple.

"Back off, or I'll kill him!" he shouted just as Guido used his head like a wrecking ball and smashed it into his captor's face. The man staggered, and Guido fell to the porch, giving the officers a clear shot at his captor. Sally Blaisedale shot the man who had been holding Guido. The other man dropped his weapon and threw his hands up. Two officers grabbed him and dragged him off the porch.

Sally ripped the ski mask off the dead man. Then she frowned.

"I've seen this man before, Gordon. He was guarding Leon Golden's estate."

Before Rawls could reply, someone inside the house started shooting. Glass shards and bullets sprayed out of the front window. Everyone on the porch ducked for cover.

As soon as she was out of range, Sally grabbed a bullhorn.

"Mr. Unger, this is Detective Sally Blaisedale. I met you at your headquarters. I was with Bridget Fournier, a deputy district attorney, and my partner, Detective Rawls."

Sally waited for an answer, but Unger didn't respond.

"Max, the house is surrounded. Your men are either in custody or dead. We don't want any more casualties. If you and your men come out, unarmed, no one else will get hurt."

Sally waited for a response. Several minutes passed. Then a man shouted, "We're coming out! Don't shoot!"

The door opened, and two men walked out with their hands up. Neither man was Max Unger.

"Where is Unger?" Gordon Rawls asked the prisoners.

Before they could answer, he heard a shot.

"Oh, shit," Rawls said as he entered the house with his gun pointing the way. It wasn't necessary. When Rawls peeked around the entrance to the living room, he saw Max Unger sitting in an armchair with a bullet hole in his temple.

"FUCK, FUCK, FUCK," SAID BRIDGET FOURNIER, WHO RARELY SWORE, when Sally Blaisedale phoned her from the farm. "I don't believe this. First Hall and Makarov. Now Unger. Everyone we thought we could turn ends up dead."

"This is disappointing," Charlie said. "But there may be a silver lining."

"I don't see one."

"Guido almost died, Bridget. Maybe this will tip him over the edge and convince him to give you the flash drive."

Bridget shook her head. "He'll take his survival as more proof of divine intervention."

CHAPTER THIRTY-FIVE

A MEDIC TREATED GUIDO AT THE FARM. THEN HE WAS TAKEN TO THE hospital in an ambulance. The good news was that Guido's jaw was not broken. The bad news was that his nose was broken, his split lip required stitches, and there was some damage to his right eye.

Charlie called Henry Roman and told him what had happened at Sabatini's farm. Roman sounded concerned, but Charlie wasn't sure if Roman was worried about their client or upset that the kidnapping had failed. In any event, Charlie was relieved that Roman was still in California, because he didn't want his cocounsel anywhere near Guido until he was certain that Roman wasn't involved in Leon Golden's sex trafficking ring.

Sally Blaisedale made certain that Guido had a guard outside his hospital room around the clock. The next morning, Guido's doctor said he could be interviewed, and Sally notified Charlie, who sat next to his client while Sally and Gordon Rawls debriefed him about what had happened at the farm before he was rescued.

Blaisedale and Rawls were very professional, and they didn't ask for any information that could have compromised Guido at his murder trial. As a result, Charlie only objected to a few questions.

When they had discussed what they wanted to cover, the detectives left Charlie alone with his client. Charlie waited to speak until Guido had taken a few sips from a glass of water. He moved his chair so he could look directly at his client and waited until he had Guido's full attention.

"I am through fucking around, Guido. This 'It's for me to know and you to find out' and 'God is protecting me' bullshit has got to stop. People are trying to kill you, and dumb luck, not the Holy Spirit, is responsible for you being alive. You also don't seem to realize that good people have died or been injured trying to protect you. If you don't turn over what you stole from Gretchen Hall's safe, I'm through with you.

"When I leave this room, I will either be your ex-lawyer or I will be on my way to Bridget Fournier's office to tell her that you are going to turn over the evidence that holds the key to putting a group of perverts behind bars where they deserve to be. So, Guido, what's it going to be?"

Guido tried to smile, but his stitches pulled, and he grimaced. "I am so fortunate to have you as my attorney, Charlie Webb. It is further proof that God watches over me."

Charlie started to speak, but Guido held up his hand.

"I have decided to follow your advice. When I am discharged from the hospital, I will give up the flash drive I took from the safe. But I have a few conditions."

"What are they?"

"I will reveal them in Judge Noonan's chambers the next time we are in court."

CHARLIE TRIED TO GET GUIDO TO TELL HIM THE CONDITIONS AND REVEAL where he was keeping the flash drive, but Guido wouldn't budge. When Charlie returned to his office, he was relieved that his client might soon be out of danger, but frustrated by his obstinacy.

He closed his office door and called Bridget Fournier.

"I might have really good news that may help you forget Unger's suicide," he said.

"I hear a lot of qualifiers in that sentence. Are you telling me that you may have news, but I shouldn't get too excited?"

"Exactly. Leonardo da Vinci's protégé has decided to turn over the item he took from Hall's safe."

"And?"

"He has conditions that will have to be met."

"Like demanding that his artwork be displayed in the Louvre?" Bridget asked.

"That sounded sarcastic."

"I'm not going to get my hopes up, Charlie. So, what are the conditions?"

"He wouldn't tell me, but he promised to lay them out in Judge Noonan's chambers as soon as he's discharged from the hospital."

"When will that be?"

"His doctors told me he'll be out tomorrow. That's why I'm calling. Can you rustle up protection for the trip to the courthouse? After what's already happened, you shouldn't have much trouble justifying a request for an armed escort."

"I'll talk to Sally and get back to you."

"I'll want a quid pro quo if you get the flash drive."

"What do you have in mind?"

"You know Guido didn't kill anyone. He's the obvious victim of a frame. A guy with a super-genius IQ isn't going to leave one of his paintings at the scene of a murder and keep the murder weapon in his house, where any half-ass search would lead to its discovery."

"You want us to dismiss the murder charges?"

"Be honest. You only indicted Guido to pressure him into giving you the flash drive."

"You're getting cynical in your old age."

"I'm just practicing the logic lessons I learned in the philosophy class I took in my junior year."

"Let me think. I'll get back to you when I've decided."

"Keep your fingers crossed. This time tomorrow, you might have the key to winning your sex trafficking case."

Moments after Charlie ended his call to Bridget, Elin walked in.

"What happened at the farm?"

"Max Unger sent men to kidnap Guido so he could find out where Guido is hiding the flash drive. This time, the police were ready, and they stopped Unger and his men cold. We had enough evidence on Unger to send him away forever, which gave us a massive bargaining chip. But it all went down the drain because Unger killed himself."

"Oh no!"

"With Unger dead, it looked like we were back to square one. Without the flash drive, Bridget only has the word of some teenage girls that Golden kidnapped them and forced them to have sex. But all may not be lost. I had a heart-to-heart with Guido. I told him that I was going to quit being his lawyer if he didn't stop jerking everyone around and turn over the drive."

"Did he agree?"

Charlie smiled. "I think so. He says he has conditions, but he'll turn over the drive if we meet them."

"What are the conditions?" Elin asked excitedly.

"To paraphrase one of our client's favorite phrases, 'That's for him to know and us to find out.'"

CHAPTER THIRTY-SIX

AS SOON AS GUIDO WAS DISCHARGED FROM THE HOSPITAL, GUIDO and Charlie were driven to the Multnomah County Courthouse in a motorcade surrounded by armed police officers. The cars stopped next to a rear courthouse entrance, and an armored and helmeted SWAT team surrounded Guido and Charlie as they got out of their car. The protective detail hustled the lawyer and his client into an elevator that took them to the floor where Judge Noonan held court.

As soon as Charlie alerted Bridget Fournier that Guido was prepared to turn over the flash drive, she had told Sally Blaisedale, Gordon Rawls, and Thomas Grant. Henry Roman was back from San Francisco, and he was waiting with the detectives and the prosecutors in the judge's chambers when Charlie and Guido walked in. Everyone looked nervous. Charlie wondered who was anxious to get the evidence that would expose the participants in a monstrous crime and who was worried about being exposed.

"Good morning, Mr. Sabatini," Judge Noonan said. "I've been

briefed about your narrow escape at your farm. How are you feeling?"

"Thank you for your concern, Judge Noonan. As you can see, I am not as handsome as I have been in my previous appearances in your honorable court, but I am healing nicely and should be able to paint again quite soon."

"Good to hear. And now I understand you have decided to give the authorities an item you took from Gretchen Hall's safe."

"Mr. Webb has convinced me that, with the exception of the miscreants whose identities will be revealed, it is in everyone's best interest for me to do so."

"I also understand that you have conditions that must be met before you will give the item you took from the safe to the authorities."

"I do."

"What are your conditions?" Judge Noonan asked.

"It has become obvious that powerful people want to destroy the flash drive I took from Gretchen Hall's safe. Numerous attempts have been made to kidnap me so I could be forced to reveal the drive's location. It has also become obvious that one or more of these powerful people may be involved in my trial."

"Now, wait one minute," Thomas Grant said. "Are you accusing me or someone in my office or the police of being involved in these kidnapping attempts?"

"I am just stating the obvious. So, I have decided that I will turn over the drive to the only people I trust besides Mr. Webb." Guido turned to Judge Noonan. "I will turn over the flash drive to you at my farm tomorrow at five o'clock."

"You want me to come to your farm?" the judge said, obviously surprised.

"You and one other person must come. No one else can be present."

"That makes no sense, Guido," Charlie said. "There are still people who want to kill you."

"I am aware of that, and the authorities can post guards all around my farm. But I will only turn over the drive to Judge Noonan in my barn tomorrow afternoon."

"You just said that there is another person who has to be present. Who is that?" Bridget asked.

Guido smiled. "The charming Miss Elin Crane."

"WHAT?!" ELIN CRANE EXCLAIMED WHEN THEY WERE IN CHARLIE'S OFFICE with the door closed.

"He said that he won't give the flash drive to Judge Noonan if you aren't there," Charlie said.

"But why? I only met him that one time, at his farm, and that didn't go very well."

"I know. I gave up trying to figure out our client a long time ago. Guido is a wack job. He operates in a universe that only parallels ours. But that begs the question. Will you go?"

"I sort of have to, don't I? The flash drive may be the key to busting Golden's sex trafficking ring."

Elin paused. She looked worried. "Will I be in any danger?"

"I'd be lying if I told you that you won't be. The people we think are named on the drive are desperate. But there will be a huge police presence around the farm, and you should be safe."

"'Should be' is not what I wanted to hear."

Charlie put his hands on Elin's shoulders and looked in her eyes. His heart was beating double time in his chest, and his throat was dry.

"If I thought that the police couldn't protect you, I'd tell you to refuse to go, no matter the consequences." Charlie swallowed. "It would kill me if anything happened to you."

Elin stared back at Charlie. She could feel him shaking. Then she leaned forward and kissed him. Charlie was stunned. Then he let nature take over.

"God, I've wanted to tell you how I feel about you since the first time you were in my office," Charlie said when they came up for air.

Elin touched Charlie's cheek, and he felt an electric charge go through him.

"I'll go," Elin said.

Charlie opened a drawer in his desk and took out a small handgun he'd gotten from Gary Schwartz. Elin stared at the weapon.

"What's that for?"

"It's for you. This is small enough to hide on your person when you go to the farm."

"I . . . Charlie, I don't want it. I've never had a gun. I'd end up shooting myself."

"It's not that difficult, Elin. You just point and shoot."

Elin laughed. "I appreciate why you think I should have it, but I don't want it. The only time I would need it is if the bad guys were able to fight their way through a squad of highly trained police. What chance do you think I'd have against mercenaries who were skilled enough to do that?"

Charlie blushed. "You make a good point."

Elin touched Charlie's cheek again. "I appreciate the gesture and your belief that I could take on a battalion of trained ninjas, but I'm going to pass on the gun."

CHAPTER THIRTY-SEVEN

GUIDO HAD TOLD BRIDGET FOURNIER THAT HE DID NOT WANT ANY POLICE closer than one hundred yards to his barn, and the police had deployed in a circle around the barn at that distance.

Judge Noonan was driven to the farm in a car with a police escort, and Charlie and Elin were in a separate car that was part of the motorcade. The cars stopped when they reached the one-hundred-yard perimeter, and the judge, Elin, and Charlie got out. Charlie could see that Elin was very nervous.

"You're going to be okay," Charlie told Elin.

"I'd feel a lot safer if you were with me," Elin said.

Charlie smiled. "Now who's being unrealistic? I'd have as much chance against a battalion of ninjas as you would."

Judge Noonan walked over to Elin. "I don't believe we've met, Miss Crane."

"No, sir."

"Do you have any idea why Mr. Sabatini wants you here?"

"I haven't a clue."

"Then let's go find out."

The judge headed toward the barn, and Elin followed him. When they walked inside, Guido was working on a painting of the Ponte Vecchio. He turned from his easel and smiled.

"Thank you for coming. Possessing this flash drive has been a burden that I will be pleased to transfer to someone else."

"Is the drive here?" the judge asked.

"No. It is in a safe place."

Noonan frowned. "Then why are we here?"

"I will answer that question after you roll up the sleeve on your right arm."

"What?"

"Do me that small favor and I will answer your question."

The judge rolled up his sleeve, exposing a tattoo of a dragon that had been inked on when he was a marine.

"Thank you, Judge."

"Okay. Mr. Sabatini, what is going on? I have never appreciated your stunts, and you are trying my patience."

"I apologize for being mysterious. So, I will tell you why I wanted you two here. I took the flash drive because I was curious. Why would Miss Hall keep such a thing in her safe? I had no interest in her money, and everything else in the safe was too bulky to take while I was carrying my wonderful painting of Venice. But the drive fit in my pocket, and I hoped it would be a bargaining chip I could use to force Miss Hall to do the right thing and hang my painting in the dining room of La Bella Roma, where all who dined there could appreciate it."

"Please get to it," Judge Noonan said, unable to hide his impatience.

"Of course, Your Honor. Once I was home, I viewed the contents of the drive." Guido looked at the judge. "It was very disturbing, especially the section that shows in graphic detail the rape and murder of a lovely young woman."

Judge Noonan stiffened.

"The killer wears a mask and nondescript clothing to hide his identity, but there is a brief moment when the sleeve of his right arm slides back to reveal a tattoo that is identical to your tattoo—a tattoo I saw when I was in your courtroom on a day you wore a short-sleeve shirt under your judicial robe."

Judge Noonan took out a gun and pointed it at Guido. "The rumors about your elevated IQ are not exaggerated, Mr. Sabatini. But you are too smart for your own good. I'm going to kill you—after you tell me where I can find the flash drive."

"Aren't you worried that Miss Crane will tell the police what you've done?" asked Guido, who was perfectly calm.

Noonan turned his head toward Elin. "I'm afraid she'll have to die—"

The judge never finished his sentence. Guido stepped forward and knocked the arm holding the gun away from him while simultaneously reversing his paintbrush. The end on the side away from the bristles had been shaved down to a very sharp point, which Guido drove into the judge's eye.

Noonan screamed. His hands flew to his eye, the gun fell to the ground, and Guido knocked him unconscious with a powerful blow to the head.

When Guido turned toward Elin, she was pointing Noonan's gun at him.

Guido smiled. "You won't have to threaten me to find out where I've hidden the flash drive. I invited you here to tell you where it is."

"Why me?"

Guido's smile widened. "There's no need to keep up your pretense of innocence, Miss Crane. I know you killed Miss Hall, Mr. Makarov, and the poor man whose body was found in the woods.

"After viewing the snuff film on the flash drive, I concluded that you were fully justified in killing Miss Hall and Mr. Makarov. I suspect that you did that for revenge. But you also had a reason for draping my painting over Miss Hall's body. You wanted to frame me for her murder. You thought that I would be forced to give the flash drive to the authorities if I was arrested. Then they could use it to prosecute Leon Golden and the men who abused all of those young women.

"I don't hold that against you. Framing me was for a good cause. I also appreciated the fact that you did away with Brent Atkins, although your effort was unnecessary. I would have been able to deal with Mr. Atkins quite easily without killing him. I suspect that you killed Mr. Atkins to protect me. If I were dead, no one would be able to find the flash drive. When I saw you on my security camera, I didn't know what you were up to, so I fled because I thought you posed the real threat."

"How did you know I killed Hall and Makarov?"

"The first time I saw you, I thought I recognized you, but I didn't remember seeing you before. Then it came to me. You have a very strong resemblance to the young woman who Judge Noonan killed in the snuff film. Is she a relative?"

"My younger sister. Are you going to tell the police?"

"Of course not. You will explain that the judge tried to kill us, but I thwarted his plan. Before we summon the authorities, there are one or two things that I would like to know. How did you lure Miss Hall to Tryon Creek park?"

"I told her I had the flash drive and I would give it to her in exchange for fifty thousand dollars."

"But how did you know about the flash drive?"

"I broke into Leon Golden's mansion and planted listening devices."

"You know how to do that?"

"I know a lot of things," Elin said as she used her blouse to wipe her fingerprints off the gun before handing it to Guido. "You take this. I don't want it."

"Thank you."

"How are you going to explain why you wanted me here?"

"That's easy. You're the only person I could be certain was not part of Leon Golden's criminal enterprise. And I needed a witness to back up my version of why I had to maim a circuit court judge."

"Do you intend to turn over the flash drive to the authorities?"

"Most definitely. It has caused me to miss too much time from my painting."

"Where is it?"

Guido laughed. "I believe you will find the answer to that question quite amusing." He stopped smiling and gestured toward Judge Noonan, who was starting to moan. "I think it's time to summon the authorities to pick up the garbage."

Elin ran out of the barn. "Come quick, and get an ambulance. Judge Noonan is badly injured."

Sally Blaisedale ran toward Elin with her gun out. "Did Sabatini attack him?" the detective asked.

"It's Noonan. He attacked us. He's on the flash drive. He's the killer in the snuff film."

Charlie ran up to Elin. "Are you okay?"

"I'm fine, thanks to Mr. Sabatini. He saved my life."

Charlie walked into the barn and stopped dead when he saw Judge Noonan writhing on the floor of the barn with a paintbrush sticking out of his eye socket.

"Jesus, Guido, did you do this?" Charlie asked.

Guido smiled. "Just because I dress like the son of God, it doesn't mean that I believe in turning the other cheek."

The detectives had made sure that there would be an ambulance near Guido's farm. While the EMTs tended to Judge Noonan, Guido told Detectives Blaisedale and Rawls why there was a paintbrush sticking out of the judge's eye.

At first, his story was met with disbelief, but Elin backed him up. By the time the judge was in an ambulance under guard headed to a hospital, the detectives were almost willing to accept Guido's assertion that Noonan was a rapist and murderer.

"The only problem we're having," Sally Blaisedale said, "is your claim that you can see Noonan's tattoo in the snuff film on the flash drive. You have to give the drive to us if you want us to accept your version of what happened in the barn."

"Of course. The flash drive will provide incontrovertible proof that His Honor is a perverted murderer."

"Are you through playing games?" Charlie asked. "Where is the flash drive?"

"You have it," Guido said.

"I do not," Charlie answered emphatically.

"You have had it for some time. You just didn't know it. Let's go to your office."

CHAPTER THIRTY-EIGHT

DETECTIVES GORDON RAWLS AND SALLY BLAISEDALE, MULTNOMAH County district attorney Thomas Grant, Deputy District Attorney Bridget Fournier, and Elin Crane followed Guido Sabatini into Charlie Webb's tiny office. As soon as everyone was inside, Guido walked over to the painting he'd given Charlie and took it off the wall. Then he turned it over and removed the backing. Nestled against the back of the canvas was the flash drive.

"I will be glad to repair the damage I have just caused," Guido told Charlie as he handed the flash drive to Sally Blaisedale.

"Please, Guido," Charlie said. "I really like that painting, and I've gotten used to seeing it every day."

"Say no more. I will take it back to my farm, and it will be gracing your wall again before the week is out."

"Thank you for protecting this evidence," Bridget told Guido. Then she turned to Charlie and smiled. "Thank you for everything you've done. It was above and beyond the call of duty."

"You can thank me and Guido by dropping the charges against him," Charlie said.

"Consider it done," Thomas Grant said.

"May I return to my painting?" Guido asked.

"I'll have a patrol car take you back," Sally said. "We're keeping a guard at the farm until we're certain that you're safe."

"I appreciate your interest in my safety," Guido said.

"Charlie, we're going to take the drive to the crime lab and have a tech open it," Sally said. "I can't tell you how much we've appreciated your help."

Charlie blushed. "I was doing it for my client."

"Well, you did a bang-up job."

Guido left, and the detectives and the prosecutors followed him out of Charlie's office. Only Charlie and Elin remained.

"Are you okay?" Charlie asked.

Elin shivered. "I'm going to see that paintbrush sticking out of the judge's eye socket in my nightmares."

"Do you want to go somewhere and get a drink?"

"Don't take this the wrong way, Charlie, but all I want to do right now is take a shower and go to bed. I'm freaked out and wiped out."

Charlie masked his disappointment. "I can understand that. I didn't feel much like socializing after my near-death experience at Guido's farm."

"Thanks for being so understanding. I'll see you tomorrow."

Elin left, and Charlie sat down behind his desk. He was alone, and he felt empty after all the excitement. He understood why Elin wanted to go home, but he had hoped that the end of Guido's case would be the start of their romance.

Charlie sighed. It wasn't as if Elin was gone forever. He would see her tomorrow. All the same, he would have liked to be with Elin tonight, instead of being alone.

CHAPTER THIRTY-NINE

AFTER ELIN LEFT HIS OFFICE, CHARLIE THOUGHT ABOUT GOING HOME, but he was too sad about Elin's quick departure and still wound up because of the events at the farm. He decided to seek comfort with his friends at the Buccaneer Tavern, and he drank beer with Gary Schwartz and Bob Malone until he ran the risk of a drunk driving conviction if he didn't stop.

It was almost ten when he walked into his apartment. He'd been thinking about Elin when he was driving home, and he was worried. She was only working on Guido's case, and it was over for all intents and purposes. He wondered what he could do to keep her in the office. Guido's was his only big case. He'd hoped that the publicity would bring in bigger cases, but no one had hired him so far. If he didn't get a big retainer soon, he wouldn't be able to pay his bills.

He decided that he had to call Elin to see how she was doing. He opened his phone and found her number in his contacts. He pressed Call, and a robotic voice told him that the number had been disconnected. That was puzzling. Then he noticed that he had a new email. He smiled. Elin must have had ESP, because the email was from her. He opened it and stopped smiling. The body of the email had a message that made Charlie dizzy. Elin had written, "I'm sorry."

There was an attachment. Charlie clicked on it. It was a voicemail.

"Hey, sis, just wanted to tell you that I'm really excited. I met this woman, Gretchen, at a club. She knows Leon Golden, the movie producer. Anyway, I'm going to his place to audition for a part in his next film. Wish me luck. I'll let you know what happens, and you get to go to the Academy Awards as my special guest when I get my Oscar."

Charlie stared at the screen. He couldn't breathe. When he was able to focus, he ran down to his car and drove through a downpour to the home address Elin had given him.

When he drove around Portland, he often wondered if a fairy had flown over the city sprinkling magic condo dust, because every few blocks contained bulldozed lots surrounded by chain-link fences where, months later, condominiums with ground-floor commercial space suddenly appeared.

He used his GPS to find the fastest route to Elin's apartment. When the GPS told him that he had arrived, he found himself in front of one of those ubiquitous vacant lots. He tried to convince himself that he'd transposed a number, but he knew that wasn't the reason he couldn't find where Elin lived.

Rain pelted the roof of his car like gunshots, but he didn't hear a thing. There was only one explanation he could think of for the false address, disconnected phone, and the email with its voicemail attachment. Elin had lied to him about everything, and her reason for lying was obvious now that he'd heard the voicemail. Elin's sister was one of Leon Golden's victims, and Elin had fooled Charlie so she could get close to Guido to convince him to turn over the flash drive.

Charlie sat in his car in a daze. Then he dialed Bridget Fournier.

"Something just happened," he said when the prosecutor picked up. "I have to see you immediately, and I absolutely have to see the snuff film."

"It's the middle of the night, Charlie. What's so important?"

"I think Elin Crane is going to murder Leon Golden."

CHAPTER FORTY

A LIGHT RAIN HAD BEGUN TO FALL SHORTLY AFTER ELIN LEFT THE MAIN highway on her way to Leon Golden's estate. By the time she arrived at the main gate, thick drops were falling hard and fast, and she was forced to turn her windshield wipers to high.

There was no guard in the sentry box, but there was a speaker affixed to the stone wall on one side of the gate. Elin lowered her window. The wind blew thick drops into the car, and she leaned back after she pressed the button at the base of the speaker. No one answered, so she pressed the button again. After the third try, she heard static and Leon Golden's voice. His speech was slurred, and she suspected that he wasn't sober.

"Who are you, and what do you want?" Golden asked.

There was a security camera mounted above the speaker. Elin looked at it and flashed a winning smile as she held up a business card she'd printed.

"Hi, Mr. Golden. I'm Elin Crane, Charlie Webb's assistant. He wanted me to tell you about an important event that happened this afternoon."

"What event?"

"Can I please come up? It's raining cats and dogs, and I'm getting soaked."

There was dead air for a minute. Then Elin heard a buzzing sound, and the gate swung open.

Elin had been prepared to see guards patrolling Golden's estate, but the guards Max Unger's National Security company had supplied were nowhere to be found. Charlie had told her that some of those guards had been killed or arrested at Guido's farm. She guessed that the rest had left as soon as they learned that their employer had committed suicide.

After Elin parked in front of Golden's house, she dashed through the rain to the front door. She had just ducked under the portico when the door swung open and Leon Golden stepped aside to let her in.

The only time she'd seen Golden was on news programs in the shots of his arrest at the Oscars. The man who admitted Elin to his mansion bore little resemblance to the nattily dressed sophisticate who had been interviewed on the red carpet. His face was covered with several days of gray-black stubble, his eyes were bloodshot, and he was wearing a warm-up suit that was decorated with food and coffee stains. When he spoke, Elin had to use all her self-control to keep from ducking away from stale breath that reeked of alcohol.

"What's this about?" Golden demanded.

CHAPTER FORTY-ONE

CHARLIE MADE A BRIEF STOP AT HIS OFFICE BEFORE DRIVING TO THE district attorney's office. It was dark after hours, and Bridget met him in reception.

"Did you send police to Golden's estate?" Charlie asked as Bridget escorted him through a maze of cubicles to her office.

Bridget nodded. "As soon as you told me why you thought he was in danger."

As soon as her door was closed and they were seated, Bridget showed Charlie the snuff film. Charlie felt sick when it ended. Bridget handed him a bottle of water, and he sipped it while he got his emotions under control.

"I found it really hard to take too," she said.

"You see the resemblance?" Charlie asked.

"I do, and the voicemail makes the identity of Noonan's victim very clear. So," Bridget asked, "who is 'Elin Crane'? After your call, I searched every database I could think of, and no Elin Crane matched your friend."

Charlie took a plastic bag out of his attaché case. There were three sheets of paper in it. Charlie handed the plastic bag to Bridget.

"I tried to find anything that might have Elin's fingerprints on it. She was using an office in my suite, but it looks like she wiped down every surface. Then I remembered that she gave me a memo with her notes about her meeting with Guido. Her prints might be on it."

"Good thinking, Charlie. I'll have the lab take a look at it."

Charlie shook his head. "I've been a fool," he said.

Bridget put a hand on his shoulder. "She fooled everyone. No one had any reason to suspect her."

"Do you think she murdered Hall and Makarov?"

"Do you have any doubts?" Bridget asked.

"No."

"She killed Brent Atkins too. They ran ballistics tests on the bullet that killed Atkins, and it came from the same gun that was used in Tryon Creek."

"I know she killed all those people, but . . ."

Bridget flashed a humorless smile. "If this were a movie, you just wouldn't cast her as a mass murderer."

Charlie laughed. "You got me." He shook his head. "I really liked her."

"You know why she did it."

"Oh yeah," Charlie said. "Vigilante justice for murdering her sister. I know I shouldn't say this, but in a way, I hope she gets away."

"I can see why you'd think that, but that's not going to happen. We'll figure out who she is, and we'll get her."

"What did you find on the flash drive besides the snuff film?" Charlie asked.

"What we thought we'd find. Graphic videos of men having sex with very young girls. A lot of the faces are familiar."

"Was anyone involved in Guido's trial on the drive?"

"Henry Roman. We're getting an arrest warrant for him."

"I was worried about Henry," Charlie said.

"I think Noonan wanted to make sure Guido would get out of custody, and he needed the best lawyer in Oregon—no offense, Charlie—on the case so granting bail would look legit."

"What about Tom Grant?"

"He wasn't on the drive, and I'm not surprised. He's got a pretty solid marriage, and someone with his ambitions has got to avoid scandals."

"I can give you a long list of politicians who didn't."

Bridget smiled. "Point taken. But Tom isn't on the drive."

Charlie yawned. "Sorry."

"Don't be. This has been a long day for both of us. Do you want a cup of our awful office coffee so you can stay awake long enough to learn what Sally and Gordon find at Golden's estate?"

CHAPTER FORTY-TWO

THREE PATROL CARS FOLLOWED DETECTIVES BLAISEDALE AND RAWLS through a driving rain to Leon Golden's estate. When they arrived at the wall that blocked access to Golden's mansion, the detectives found the gate open.

"That can't be good," Rawls said.

"Agreed," Blaisedale said before keying in the radio that connected her to the follow cars.

"Everyone, on your toes. Elin Crane is very dangerous. Do not hesitate to shoot her if you're threatened. Remember, she has already murdered three people."

Golden's mansion came in sight. Sally grew uneasy.

"The last time I was here, guards were patrolling the grounds.

"I see a car parked near the front door," Sally said. "I'm going to park here and go the rest of the way on foot. If Crane is in there, the rain may cover our approach."

Sally signaled a halt. The other cars stopped, and the officers got out. Sally unholstered her sidearm and checked it. Then she moved toward the house with the others behind her. The front door was open, and rain was blowing in, drenching the entryway. Sally raced into the house with two officers close behind. She saw Leon Golden sprawled on the floor with a gun in his hand just as she heard an officer scream, "Runner!"

Sally ran outside, and an officer pointed toward the side of the house. When Sally rounded the corner, she saw a figure racing toward the forest that surrounded the estate. The rain was falling in sheets, and that made it hard to see if the person was a man or a woman, but Sally thought her prey looked slender enough and tall enough to be Elin Crane.

"Get her before she makes it into the trees!" Rawls shouted.

Sally ran distance to stay in shape, and she began to close the gap between herself and the fleeing figure. Then, just as she and two of the officers got close, Elin turned and fired. Sally hit the ground. When she looked up, Crane had disappeared into the woods.

Sally swore and got to her feet. She ran forward, cautious now that she knew that Crane was armed. When she reached the first line of trees, she slowed down and walked through it slowly with her gun leading the way.

She heard the officers crashing through the trees on either side. The canopy brought some relief from the downpour, but Sally was soaked when she walked into a small clearing. She turned slowly, worried that Crane could be hiding anywhere in the trees and underbrush that encircled her. When she didn't see any movement, she edged between two trees in a line toward the last path she'd seen Crane take.

Just as Sally moved out of the clearing, an arm circled her throat, and a hard chop on her wrist knocked her gun to the ground. Seconds later, she was thrown down, and a gun barrel screwed into her temple.

"Don't try to yell or I'll have to hurt you," Elin whispered. "I only shot at you so I could get into these woods, and I shot over your head. I don't want to hurt you or any of the officers."

"I understand why you killed Hall and Makarov," Sally said. "We've seen the snuff film. Turn yourself in and we can work a deal where you get a lighter sentence."

Crane laughed. "If I let you take me in, I'll be facing multiple homicide charges. Those scum deserved to die for what they did to my sister and all the other girls, but I know enough law to know that I'm not going to get a slap on the wrist.

"But enough small talk. You're going to lead me back to your car, and we're going to drive away. When I'm safe, I'll let you out. Help me and you'll live."

Elin pulled Sally to her feet and used the detective's cuffs to secure her hands behind her back. Then she kept behind Blaisedale as she steered the detective through the woods in a circuitous route that took them onto the road behind the parked cars.

Two officers were standing near the front door, and they started to walk toward Crane and the detective.

"Ask them how Golden is doing," Elin whispered.

"How is Golden doing?" Sally yelled.

"He's alive. We sent for an ambulance," one of the officers said.

"Tell them to go inside and wait for the ambulance to come," Elin said.

Sally repeated what Crane had said. The officers, who were

only too pleased to get out of the rain, went back inside Golden's mansion.

When they reached Sally's ride, Crane took Sally's keys and put her in the passenger seat. Then she looped Blaisedale's seat belt around her.

"Don't try anything foolish and you'll be okay," Elin said as she drove into the night.

AN AMBULANCE WAS PARKED IN FRONT OF LEON GOLDEN'S MANSION by the time Gordon Rawls and the other officers gave up the search for Elin Crane. Rawls was soaked to the skin and only too glad to get out of the rain. As soon as he entered Golden's home, he spotted two EMTs working on Golden, who was sprawled across the floor. He was alive but leaking blood from a shattered kneecap. An officer was holding an evidence bag that contained a handgun.

Rawls talked to the EMTs, who were getting ready to put Golden on a stretcher. Then he watched as Golden was transported to the ambulance. As he looked around the entryway, it dawned on Rawls that he didn't see his partner.

"Anyone seen Detective Blaisedale?" he asked.

"Yeah," one of the officers said. "She and another person came out of the woods, a little before everyone else. She asked how Mr. Golden was doing. Then she told me to go inside and wait for the ambulance."

"She was with someone else?" Rawls asked.

"Yeah. They were going to the car you drove in."

"Was the other person a police officer?"

"It was raining hard and the other person was standing behind Detective Blaisedale, so I couldn't see who it was."

Rawls got an icy feeling in his gut. He walked out of the house and toward the spot where his and Blaisedale's ride had been parked. The car was gone. Rawls raced to one of the patrol cars and put out an all-points bulletin for a stolen police car.

CHAPTER FORTY-THREE

BRIDGET LEFT TO GET THE COFFEE, AND CHARLIE CLOSED HIS EYES. HE thought about Elin. He should be furious at the way she'd played him for a fool, but it was hard to stay angry when he thought about why she'd tricked him into making her part of Guido's defense team. He wondered what he'd do if he had a sister who was raped and murdered for entertainment and he knew the identity of the person who had murdered her.

A hand on Charlie's shoulder jerked him awake, and he saw Bridget looking down at him. He realized that he must have drifted off. He flushed with embarrassment.

"Sorry," he apologized.

"No need. When I came back with the coffee, you were out like a light. I decided to let you get your beauty sleep until I got intel from Golden's estate."

Suddenly, Charlie was wide awake. "Did Sally call you?"

"No, but Gordon Rawls did. Elin sent us Leon Golden's confession."

"That's great!"

"There's a problem. She shot him before he made it, so his lawyer is going to scream that it was coerced.

"And there's one very big and very scary problem. Gordon thinks that Elin kidnapped Sally Blaisedale."

CHARLIE THOUGHT ABOUT GOING HOME, BUT THE NEWS ABOUT ELIN Crane and Sally Blaisedale had bummed him out. Charlie called Gary and Bob and asked them to meet him at the Buccaneer Tavern. They were waiting with two pitchers of beer and three mugs. Charlie made a dent in one pitcher while he brought the Barbarians up to date.

"Jesus, Charlie, you sure know how to pick 'em," Gary Schwartz said when Charlie told them that Elin had killed Gretchen Hall, Yuri Makarov, and Brent Atkins and crippled Leon Golden.

"Don't rub it in," Charlie said. "I feel bad enough as it is."

"You really liked her, didn't you?" Bob asked.

"She always seemed to be out of my league, but I was hoping that something would happen."

"She didn't kill you," Gary said. "So, she must have felt something for you."

"Thanks, Gary, for seeing the silver lining in this mega-fucked-up situation."

Bob wrapped his arm around Charlie's shoulder. "We love you, Charlie."

"Thanks, Bob. I do know I can always count on you two, no matter how screwed up you are."

Gary raised his mug. "I'll drink to that."

Charlie and Bob joined him just as Charlie's phone rang. He checked the caller ID.

"Hey, Bridget, you're not still at your office, are you?"

"Are you drinking, Charlie?"

"Maybe a little."

"Well, I have some information that may sober you up. Where are you?"

"I'm at the Buccaneer Tavern with two degenerate bikers."

"Gary and Bob?"

"You guessed it."

"I'd ask you to drive downtown, but I'd have to prosecute you for DUII, so sit tight and I'll be there as quick as I can."

"GOOD EVENING, GENTLEMEN," BRIDGET SAID WHEN SHE TOOK A SEAT at the table with Charlie and the bikers.

"That's the first time anyone has ever called Gary a *gentleman*," Bob said.

"She sees the real me, asshole," Gary said.

Bob smiled at the DA. "Still think he's a gentleman?"

"I overlook the faults of anyone who saves my life, Bob. Even yours."

"Touché," Bob said with a grin.

"I didn't know you spoke French," Gary said.

"If you two are done, I'd like to hear why Bridget is here," Charlie said.

"I called in a favor at the crime lab. Carrie Stanton found prints on the memo and ran them through AFIS, the Automated Fingerprint Identification System. Alexis Chandler grew up in Scranton, Pennsylvania. She was a high school track star who went to UCLA on a track scholarship before dropping out in her sophomore year after severely injuring a man in a bar after he grabbed her breast. The DA said what she did was overkill, but her lawyer got her a deal, and the charges were dismissed when she joined the army, where she received the type of training that makes her extremely dangerous. Chandler served tours in Iraq and Afghanistan and is an expert markswoman with sniper training, very skilled in hand-to-hand combat, and she's a whiz with computers and tech."

"In other words," Gary said, "she is one dangerous mother-fucker."

"You hit the nail on the head, Gary," Bridget said. "She left the army a few years ago and went back to college to finish her degree. She was going into her senior year when Annie, her younger sister, disappeared. Annie left Alexis an excited voicemail telling her that Leon Golden was auditioning her for a part in a picture. When Golden and Hall were arrested at the Oscars, Alexis moved to Oregon and brought her skills with her. You know the rest."

Gary raised his mug. "To outlaws everywhere. May the gods watch over Alexis."

"Have you heard anything new about Sally Blaisedale?" Charlie asked.

"Yes, and it's good news. Alexis let her go near the California border. She's unharmed."

"That is good news," Charlie said.

"I've had a very long and very stressful day," Bridget told Charlie. "So, I'm heading home. You are in no condition to drive, and neither are your friends. Can I offer you a lift? You can pick up your car tomorrow."

"I'm pretty beat too, so I'll accept your kind offer." Charlie stood up, swaying a little as he did.

"Take good care of Charlie," Bob said. "Good lawyers are hard to find."

Bridget guided Charlie to her car. Charlie had to fight to keep his eyes open, and he lost the battle. When Bridget parked in front of Charlie's apartment building, she saw that her passenger was asleep. She smiled. Then she shook his shoulder. Charlie's eyes opened, and he looked lost.

"We're here. You nodded off," Bridget said.

"Gee, I'm sorry. I didn't snore, did I?"

"Fortunately, no."

Charlie straightened up and opened his door. "Thanks for babysitting me."

Bridget smiled. "You were a breeze compared to some of the brats I sat for when I was in high school."

Charlie laughed. "I appreciate you coming to the Buccaneer to bring me up to date."

"I thought you deserved to know what I found."

"Well, thanks for everything. Get a good night's sleep."

Charlie was going to say, "I'll see you tomorrow," but he stopped himself when he realized that he would probably not see Bridget now that Guido's case was over.

Bridget drove off, and Charlie made the trek up to his apartment. He shucked his clothes in the hallway, shuffled into the bathroom, then dropped into bed. But he didn't nod off right away. He thought about Alexis Chandler.

Elin Crane had been the girl of his dreams—stunningly beautiful with an amazing body and really smart. Way out of his league, and head and shoulders above anyone he'd ever dated. He'd been infatuated with her until he found out that Elin Crane was a façade behind which a duplicitous killer was hiding. He concluded that he'd thought with his dick instead of using his brain. As soon as it became clear that she was using him as part of a plan to avenge her sister, anything he felt for her had disappeared.

Now he thought about Bridget Fournier. Bridget had integrity. She was solid and trustworthy and gutsy and smart, and it dawned on him that he really liked her. He decided she was someone he'd like to know better. And he could do that, if Bridget were willing, now that Guido's case was over.

He gathered his courage and got out of bed. He guessed that Bridget had just gotten home. He found her number and called her.

"Charlie?" Bridget said when she answered.

"Uh, yeah. I didn't wake you, did I?"

"No. I was just getting ready for bed. Why are you calling?"

"Uh, I was thinking of something. You don't have to if you don't want to. But now that we're not on opposite sides of a case, I was wondering if you'd like to have dinner sometime."

Bridget laughed. "I think that would be nice, but it can't be at the Buccaneer Tavern."

"No, no. It will be at a restaurant that we mutually agree on. You can even pick the place."

"Deal. If you still want to have dinner with me when you sober up, call me in the morning."

CHAPTER FORTY-FOUR

THREE MONTHS LATER, CHARLIE STOOD IN A CROWD AT THE PORTLAND International Airport, waiting for Miriam Adler to walk onto the concourse. Charlie didn't know what Guido's mother looked like, but Miriam had seen Charlie on TV, and he towered above the other excited family members and friends who congregated in front of the exit doors.

At Charlie's urging, Guido had called Miriam. The initial phone conversation had been strained, but there had been subsequent long-distance talks that had resulted in Miriam asking if it would be okay to visit and Guido consenting.

Miriam was going to stay at the farm, and Charlie had volunteered to pick her up and drive her there so Guido wouldn't have to take time from painting.

While Charlie waited, his thoughts drifted to Alexis Chandler. Charlie and Bridget Fournier had been seeing each other, and that was going really well. Bridget kept him up to date on the hunt for Chandler, who was still at large. Alexis had been sighted in Spain, but there were also reports that she was in Chile and the Bahamas. In other words, no one knew where she was. Part of Charlie rooted for Alexis. He knew she was a killer and she had made a fool of him, but he couldn't help feeling that everything she'd done was justified—if not by the statutes of the State of Oregon, then by the biblical rule of an eye for an eye. Given the atrocities the men in Golden's sex club had committed, Charlie found it hard to condemn Alexis for avenging her sister and the other victims, a sentiment shared unanimously by Bob Malone, Gary Schwartz, and the other members of the Barbarians Motorcycle Club.

Leon Golden was singing like the proverbial canary in hopes of avoiding an indictment that charged him with being an accessory to murder. Using his information and the contents of the flash drive, the DA's office had arrested seven men. Some were prominent businessmen and politicians. The list included Anthony Noonan, who was facing a murder charge, and Henry Roman. One thing that Golden said made Charlie very sad. Alexis had asked him what happened to Annie's body. Golden said that Yuri Makarov had disposed of it, and only Makarov knew where she was. Now that Makarov was dead, it was unlikely that Annie would ever get a proper burial.

Charlie's practice was starting to pick up too, thanks to all the publicity he'd gotten from Guido's case. He wasn't raking in the dough, but he was getting enough business to justify hiring an associate, who was now using the office Elin Crane had worked in.

Miriam's plane had landed twenty minutes earlier, and a steady flow of passengers had walked into the waiting arms of the people who had turned out to greet them. Charlie watched a family of four come through the exit. They were followed by a plump woman who was barely five feet tall. She had curly black hair with a scattering of gray and soft brown eyes that were scanning the crowd. The eyes stopped when they focused on Charlie, and the woman managed a tentative smile. Charlie smiled back, and moments later, they were headed toward the baggage claim.

"How was your flight?" Charlie asked as they took the escalator down.

"It was long, but the woman next to me was very nice, and we talked through a lot of it." Miriam looked embarrassed. "I've never been on a plane before. Jerry didn't like to travel, and we didn't have a lot of extra money for vacations."

"Given the current state of air travel, you're lucky," Charlie said. "At least your flight wasn't canceled."

"That's my bag," Miriam said as she pointed to a valise that had just come out of the chute.

"No lost bags," Charlie said with a smile. "You're batting a thousand."

CHARLIE PARKED HIS CAR IN FRONT OF GUIDO'S BARN. THEN HE WENT around and opened the passenger door for Miriam Adler. He could tell Miriam was very nervous during the ride to the farm, and he tried to assure her that everything would work out, even though he wasn't completely sure. Guido was still Guido and as unpredictable and volatile as ever.

"You need to know a few things about your son," Charlie had said when they were on the highway. "First—and I have no idea how this will play out—Larry really thinks that he is Guido Sabatini, a reincarnation of a Renaissance painter who studied with Michelangelo and Leonardo da Vinci. During the time I represented him, he wouldn't respond when he was addressed as Lawrence Weiss."

Miriam smiled. "I've called him *Larry* during our phone calls, and he hasn't objected."

"That's a good sign," Charlie said. Then he hesitated before bringing up the next topic. "Ms. Adler, there's no easy way to put this, but Guido has serious mental problems. He should be seeing a psychiatrist to deal with his childhood traumas. I've suggested that he see someone, but he resists the suggestion. You should see if you can convince him to get help, but let it drop if it interferes with reestablishing your relationship.

"One final thing. Your son is a brilliant painter, and the publicity his paintings received when he was on trial have resulted in a large number of sales. You should be proud of what he's accomplished and the peace he's found through painting."

Charlie led Miriam into the barn. Guido stopped when his mother and Charlie walked in. He looked nervous.

"Hello, Larry," Miriam said.

"How was your flight?" Guido asked for something to say.

"It was fine," Miriam said. There were tears in her eyes. "I'm so glad to be here."

Guido tried to say something, but he was frozen.

"What are you working on?" Charlie asked so Guido could retreat to a safe topic.

"A pastoral scene in Tuscany at sunset. Getting the light just right is trying my patience."

"I have faith in you, Guido," Charlie said. "You'll figure it out. May we see the painting?"

Guido stepped aside, and Miriam followed Charlie to the easel.

"It's beautiful," Miriam said.

Guido smiled. "I'm glad you approve. Perhaps you will accept it as a gift?"

"I'd be honored." Miriam paused and looked at her son. "I'm so proud of you. What you do here. How many people can create such beauty?"

"Your mother has had a long flight, and I bet she's starving," Charlie said. "Why don't you show her to her room and fix her something to eat?"

"That is an excellent suggestion," Guido said, relieved to have a chore to perform that would ease the tense situation. "Follow me, Mother. I have a very pleasant guest room. You'll be the first to use it. While you're getting settled, I'll prepare some food. Will you eat a sandwich? I have homemade bread, excellent cheese, and Serrano ham."

Just before Guido took his mother into the farmhouse, Charlie told them that he had to get to his office. Miriam thanked him for driving her to the farm, and Guido thanked him for gifting him time to paint. As he drove away, Charlie thought Miriam's visit was starting out well. Guido had acted like a sane person, and Charlie hoped that the rest of Miriam's visit would be a success. He was grateful for little things where his ex-client was concerned.

When he walked into the waiting room, his receptionist told him that a Mr. Beecham had called several times.

"He says it's urgent," the receptionist said.

"That name sounds familiar."

"It should. It's all over the TV and the internet."

"Why?"

"He's the CEO of a major tech company, and his son was just arrested for drowning his wife on a fishing trip."

PART SIX
A SIGNIFICANT CASE

TWO YEARS LATER

CHAPTER FORTY-FIVE

BRIDGET FOURNIER CREPT OUT OF BED AS QUIETLY AS POSSIBLE TO avoid waking Charlie, who didn't have to be in court until one o'clock. She dressed in the walk-in closet in the condo she and Charlie had moved into three months earlier, then went into the kitchen. A few minutes later, she carried a cup of freshly brewed coffee and a toasted bagel into the dining room. Through the condo's floor-to-ceiling windows, Bridget could see the metallic green arches of the Fremont Bridge as it crossed over the Willamette River and the snowy slopes of Mount Hood, bathed in the rays of the rising sun, sights that always delighted her and helped her relax before she went into battle.

Charlie was dead to the world after getting in late. He had been prepping a witness he was going to put on to counter the expert the prosecution was using to bolster its evidence in a pretrial motion in a burglary case.

Bridget's case, a federal drug prosecution she had no chance of winning, was only being tried because the US attorney refused to plea bargain. Bridget couldn't blame him. When she was prosecuting, she probably would have done the same thing with a prosecution case this strong and a defendant this degenerate. But she wasn't a prosecutor anymore. She was a name partner in Fournier and Webb.

Bridget had started dating Charlie after the case against Guido Sabatini was dismissed. The publicity had brought Charlie a few new clients, but no case as spectacular as Guido's. Then Lloyd Beecham, the son of a multimillionaire tech CEO, made front-page news when he was charged with drowning his wife during a fishing trip. His family hired Charlie to defend a case everyone assumed he would lose. But Charlie's jury had delivered a not guilty verdict, and a flood of clients who could afford to pay healthy retainers had poured in. That's when Charlie asked Bridget to join his firm.

Accepting Charlie's offer had not been an easy decision. Bridget had spent several sleepless nights tossing and turning as she weighed the pros and cons of quitting the DA's office and representing the type of people she used to put in prison. In the end, she decided that she had been a prosecutor for almost ten years, and a new challenge sounded exciting. Not to mention that she and Charlie would be working together. As soon as Bridget accepted his offer, Charlie had given her star billing in the firm's name to show his appreciation.

The firm was doing very nicely, and they and their two associates had just moved into new digs in the same building where Henry Roman practiced before he was sentenced to serve ten years in the Oregon State Penitentiary. One of the associates was handling divorce cases, and the other one was an experienced personal injury lawyer that Charlie had lured away from a big plaintiff's firm. That let Bridget and Charlie concentrate on the criminal cases, many of which were still referrals from the Barbarians, who always got a discounted fee.

Bridget finished her breakfast, grabbed her attaché case, and left for court, closing the door quietly so Charlie could continue getting his beauty sleep.

CHARLIE HELD HIS BREATH WHEN JUDGE SARAH BELMONT BEGAN TO TELL the parties how she was going to rule on Charlie's motion to suppress. The State's forensic experts had found a set of latent prints in the house Fred Tremaine and his two schoolmates were accused of burglarizing. Fred was a tenth grader with no police record and no prints on file. After Fred was arrested, his prints had been taken when he was booked into the Multnomah County jail. At the pretrial hearing on Charlie's motion to suppress, the police expert testified that the fingerprints found in the burglarized house matched the prints taken from his client during the booking process.

Charlie had argued that his client had been illegally arrested without probable cause. If his reading of the law was correct, the judge would have to exclude the evidence of the fingerprints obtained when Fred was booked into the jail. Since the fingerprints were the only evidence linking his client to the burglary, the prosecutor would have to dismiss the case if the judge granted the motion.

"This is a close case," Judge Belmont said, "but the totality of the evidence leads me to conclude that the officers did not have probable cause when they arrested Mr. Tremaine. So, I am going to grant Mr. Tremaine's motion and exclude any mention of fingerprint evidence at his trial."

"We won," Charlie whispered to his client. Fred sagged in his chair. The prosecutor objected to the ruling and indicated that his office would appeal. Then the court went into recess.

As soon as Judge Belmont left the bench, Fred's mother hugged Charlie, and his father shook his hand. The Tremaines were wealthy residents of Lake Oswego, an upscale suburb, and solid citizens. Fred had been a good student, but he'd started hanging out with a group at school that had talked him into breaking into a house in his neighborhood. His arrest had shocked Fred. Charlie believed his client was sincere when he told him that he'd been an idiot to break into the house on a dare and was going to stay away from the other boys, who were also facing burglary charges.

Charlie walked to his office with a smile on his face. Unlike many of his clients, Fred Tremaine was a decent human being, and Charlie was glad he'd kept him from getting a criminal record that would screw up his future. The prosecutor had put on the record that he was going to appeal, but Charlie was certain that the law was on Fred's side and that the judge's decision would not be reversed.

Charlie arrived at Fournier and Webb at a little after four. Bridget was still in trial, and he didn't expect her to return to the office until after he'd left for the evening. She'd told Charlie that she'd be prepping a witness and to eat without her.

Charlie booted up his computer and checked his emails. There was nothing he couldn't handle the next day. Then he organized the Tremaine file and put it in a filing cabinet. He'd need it when the State appealed, but that wouldn't be for months.

Charlie had scarfed down a food-cart burrito on the way to the courthouse and hadn't eaten anything else. His stomach started to rumble, and he was preparing to go home when his receptionist told him that an inmate was calling from the jail.

"Is it one of our clients?" Charlie asked.

"I don't think so. It's a woman. Her name is Alexis Chandler."

The call wasn't entirely unexpected. Charlie had read about Alexis's arrest in Mexico.

"Put her through." When he was connected, he asked, "Why are you calling?"

"You're not mad at me, are you, Charlie?"

"That question can't be answered with a simple yes or no. I would need a multipage essay."

Alexis laughed. "I wouldn't blame you if you're pissed. I lied to you and used you to get to Guido."

"I've seen the snuff film, and I know why you did what you did. What I've never decided is whether you were justified in taking the law into your own hands."

"Why don't you come to the jail and we can talk about the conflict between morality and the law during a confidential attorney-client meeting."

"You want me to represent you?"

"Of course. I've been charged with a slew of violations of the criminal statutes of Oregon, including multiple counts of murder, and I need the best representation possible."

CHAPTER FORTY-SIX

CHARLIE WALKED TO THE JAIL BUFFETED BY CONFLICTING EMOTIONS. Alexis Chandler was a cold-blooded killer who had wormed her way into his confidence and betrayed his trust. But Alexis was also the avenger of a sister who had been brutally murdered for sport. What Alexis had done was legally wrong, but was it morally wrong?

The one unwavering decision he had reached by the time Alexis was led into the contact visiting room was that he wouldn't agree to take on her case until he discussed it with Bridget.

Alexis was dressed in an orange jail-issue jumpsuit, but she walked with her back straight, her shoulders back, and a welcoming smile on her face. She still had an athletic figure, but she had dyed her hair black, and the skin that had been as white as ivory was now a rich shade of brown.

"Nice tan," Charlie said, "but I liked you better as a blonde."

"I was living in a Mexican beach town, and blondes stood out. This was my disguise."

"How did they get you?" Charlie asked.

"I made a mistake and trusted the wrong person. My bad. But what's done is done, and here I am. So, are you going to represent me?"

"I'm not sure. But our conference is protected by the attorney-client privilege even if I decide I'm not going to be your lawyer, so you can speak freely."

"What are your concerns?" Alexis asked.

"Let's get the business part out of the way. Murder cases take up a lot of time and are very expensive. We're talking six, seven figures when you factor in hiring an investigator and retaining expert witnesses. Do you have that kind of money?"

"Actually, I do. My parents were well off, and they died in a car accident. Annie and I inherited."

Alexis choked up for a moment. She looked down at the metal table that separated her and the lawyer. When she'd regained her composure, she sat up and looked at Charlie. The smile with which she had greeted him had disappeared, and he saw how much suffering her sister's death still caused her.

"I can cover your fees," she said.

"Okay. What are you charged with?"

"Killing Gretchen Hall, Yuri Makarov, and Brent Atkins and shooting Leon Golden. They also tacked on a kidnapping charge because I took Detective Blaisedale with me when I escaped. There are a couple of other counts, but those are the biggies."

"Have you been interviewed by the police?"

"Detective Blaisedale's partner, Rawls, questioned me. I guess Sally can't be involved, now that she's a witness."

"What did you tell Rawls?"

Alexis smiled. "What do you think I said? The minute he asked me a question, I told him I wanted to talk to a lawyer. He tried to get me to talk anyway, but I told him that he was wasting his breath."

"That's good to hear. Even so, this isn't going to be easy. Given all of the charges, your best bet may end up being plea bargaining to avoid the death penalty on the murder charges."

"Why would I plead guilty when I'm morally justified in killing Hall and Makarov?"

"Yeah, about that. That works in fiction, but you'll be tried using the Oregon Revised Statutes. Vigilante justice isn't recognized in any of them."

"What about self-defense? That gets you off if you kill someone, doesn't it?"

ALEXIS HAD GIVEN CHARLIE A LOT TO THINK ABOUT, AND HIS THOUGHTS caromed back and forth in his brain when he left the jail. A million-dollar retainer would be great, and Alexis had given him information about what had happened that might convince a jury to acquit on some of the most serious charges, but he wasn't convinced that her version of events wasn't a complete fabrication.

That didn't bother Charlie. A defense attorney accepted any story his client told him, no matter how outrageous, because he, like the jurors, had to assume his client was as pure as the driven snow until the client admitted guilt. Charlie had actually had a few cases where he was convinced that his client was guilty when the trial started, but had changed his mind when all the evidence was in and the jury had acquitted. Those cases had convinced him that he should never prejudge a client's guilt.

The problem was Charlie's mixed emotions about his potential client and his belief that all the people in the sex trafficking scheme deserved the cruelest of punishments.

BRIDGET STAGGERED INTO THE CONDO AT NINE THIRTY. CHARLIE ASKED her how the trial was going and waited until Bridget was through venting before telling her that he'd had a very interesting day that involved a meeting with a potential client who could afford a seven-figure retainer.

"Is this someone I've read about in the newspapers?" Bridget asked as she paused between bites of an avocado, bacon, and lettuce sandwich she'd slapped together while she told Charlie about her awful day in court.

"It's actually someone you know personally."

Bridget frowned. "I'm too tired to play twenty questions. Stop being mysterious."

"Elin Crane, a.k.a. Alexis Chandler, is in the county jail charged with murder, kidnapping, assault, and several other crimes, and she wants me to represent her."

Bridget's mouth had opened so she could continue to eat, but the hand holding her sandwich froze halfway to her mouth.

"Why in the world would you want to represent a serial killer who lied to you and used you to get to one of your clients?"

"First of all, I hope you agree that every defendant, no matter how awful, deserves representation."

"Especially if they're gorgeous and have a body men drool over," Bridget answered.

Charlie turned beet red. "Please tell me that you're not jealous."

"Absolutely not!"

"I did have a crush on Elin Crane, but that went away when I learned that she used me and was a stone-cold killer."

"Then why are you giving her the time of day?"

Charlie told Bridget what Alexis had said about her defenses.

"That sounds like a load of shit," Bridget said.

"Maybe, maybe not. And remember why she went on her killing spree. You've seen the snuff film. What if that was your sister?"

Bridget remembered Annie Chandler begging for mercy as Anthony Noonan raped and strangled her. She took a deep breath.

"Do you believe that she acted in self-defense when she killed Hall, Makarov, and Atkins and shot Golden?" Bridget asked.

"I don't have to believe her to defend her. The jurors make that decision after they hear what she has to say and they judge her credibility. So, what do you think? I won't accept Alexis's case if you don't want the firm to represent her."

Bridget took a bite out of her sandwich and thought as she chewed. Charlie waited, hoping that Bridget would get on board.

"Okay," Bridget said.

CHAPTER FORTY-SEVEN

THOMAS GRANT WAS CHATTING WITH THE REPORTERS IN THE HALLWAY
outside the courtroom where Alexis Chandler was going to be arraigned when he spotted Charlie and Bridget walking toward him.

"What are you two doing here?" Grant asked.

"This is where Alexis Chandler is going to be arraigned, isn't
it?" Charlie asked.

"Don't tell me you're going to represent Chandler after she
fucked you over," Grant said.

"And good morning to you too, Tom," Charlie replied.

"She was your employee. Don't you have some kind of conflict?"

"Bridget and I talked it over, and we decided my relationship
with Alexis won't disqualify us from taking her case."

Grant chuckled. "Hey, it's your funeral. I couldn't have been
given a stronger case if I handpicked the facts myself."

"Then the trial should be a snooze for you," Charlie answered.

"If we get that far. Once you see what we've got, I expect you to run to my office to ask for a plea bargain."

"We'll see after we read the discovery in her case. Can you messenger it over to us?"

"Sure thing, Charlie. I'll even use a Magic Marker to highlight all of the evidence that proves your adorable client is, beyond a reasonable doubt, a mass murderer."

"Thanks, Tom."

Grant turned to Bridget. "We all miss you. It's a shame you went over to the dark side."

Bridget laughed. "We'd better get inside. Court should be starting."

Alexis's arrest had been front-page news, and the courtroom was packed.

"How are you holding up?" Charlie asked when the guards had taken off Alexis's shackles and she was seated next to him.

Alexis smiled. "Jail is a breeze after some of the places I was in when I served."

Charlie chuckled. "I keep forgetting you were in combat in war zones."

Alexis stopped smiling. "That's a time of my life, like this one, that I'd like to forget. What are my chances of getting bailed out?"

"That's not going to happen. There's no automatic bail in a death case, and given that you've already been hiding out in Mexico, I won't be able to argue that you aren't a flight risk."

"Then what's happening today?"

"We'll waive the reading of the indictment and enter pleas of not guilty to all the charges. Even though we won't win, I'll ask for a bail hearing so we can get some idea of the State's case, and we'll do some scheduling."

The bailiff rapped his gavel, and the Honorable Isaac Steinbock took the bench. Charlie and Bridget had been happy when they heard that Judge Steinbock had been selected to hear Alexis's case. The judge was in his late fifties, but he looked younger. He was a gym rat and had a wiry physique, a full head of curly black hair with only a smattering of gray, and bright blue eyes that were cast in shadow by bushy black eyebrows. Trying a case in Steinbock's court was a pleasant experience because he had a jovial disposition, treated the litigants with respect, and was very smart.

"Good morning, ladies and gentlemen," Judge Steinbock said after his bailiff called the case. "Are you ready to proceed?"

The parties stood.

"Thomas Grant for the People of Oregon. We're ready."

"Charlie Webb and Bridget Fournier for Miss Chandler. We're ready, and we waive a reading of the indictment."

"Very well, Mr. Webb. How does Miss Chandler plead?"

"Not guilty to all of the counts."

"Okay. What's the State's position on bail, Mr. Grant?"

"This is a murder case with no automatic bail, and the defendant has been on the run for two years, so there's no question that she's a flight risk. So, we ask the court to hold the defendant and not grant her release on bail."

"Mr. Webb?" Judge Steinbock asked.

"We'd like you to schedule a bail hearing."

"How does next Tuesday suit everybody?" the judge asked.

"We're good," Charlie said.

"Tuesday is fine with the State."

"Okay, then. If there's nothing else, we'll be in recess."

"What happens next?" Alexis asked.

"In a few weeks, a jury of your peers will decide if you live or die."

CHAPTER FORTY-EIGHT

THAT AFTERNOON, CHARLIE AND BRIDGET WERE SEATED NEXT TO EACH other in their conference room sipping caffe lattes while they pored over the discovery that Thomas Grant had sent them.

"What do you think?" Charlie asked when they'd finished reading the police reports, autopsy reports, reports from the crime lab, and viewing the crime scene photographs.

"It's the guns," Bridget said. "All of those guns."

"My thought exactly."

"We'll need an expert."

"Great minds think alike."

Bridget grinned. "You're giving yourself way more credit than your IQ tests support."

Charlie laughed. Then he got serious. "Who do we call?"

"I know just the man."

CHARLIE'S NAVIGATION SYSTEM TOLD HIM TO TAKE A RIGHT TURN INTO an industrial park that was a few blocks from the Columbia River.

Then it told him that he was eight hundred feet from his destination. Charlie parked in front of an unremarkable concrete building, locked his car, and walked up a ramp to a walkway that passed in front of an export-import business and a construction firm and ended at Oregon Forensic Investigations.

Oregon Forensic Investigations was owned by Paul Baylor, who had a degree from Michigan State University in forensic science and criminal justice and had worked at the Oregon State Crime Lab for ten years before going out on his own. He had a reputation for integrity, which he'd gotten by telling defense attorneys the truth about the evidence in their cases when that was the last thing they wanted to hear. That reputation carried a lot of weight with the district attorneys' offices in Oregon, and it was not unusual for a case to be dismissed when one of Baylor's reports was presented to the prosecution as part of a discovery package.

The door to Oregon Forensic Investigations opened into a small anteroom furnished with two chairs that flanked a table covered with old copies of scientific journals. Across from the door was a desk that no one was sitting at. Behind the desk was a sliding glass window, and next to the desk was a door. Charlie opened the door and found himself in a long room cluttered with scientific paraphernalia.

"Mr. Baylor?" Charlie shouted. "I'm Charlie Webb. We had an appointment for three o'clock."

He heard a gunshot coming from the back of the room. He called out again, and a slender, bookish African American wearing wire-rimmed glasses walked into view.

"Mr. Webb?" Paul Baylor asked.

"Hi. Are you Mr. Baylor?"

"I am, and it's Paul. On the phone, you said that you had some questions about guns and a gunshot that had been made at a crime scene."

Charlie nodded. Then he looked around at the surfaces on which he could spread out what he was carrying in his attaché case. It looked like every square foot of usable space was covered with test tubes, beakers, paperwork, and machines he could not identify.

"I have the crime scene photographs and reports in here. Is there someplace I can show them to you?"

Baylor smiled. "I apologize for the mess. I've got a lot of cases I'm juggling right now. Let's go to my office."

Baylor led the way to a corner of the large room, where an open door revealed a small, cramped office outfitted with an inexpensive desk, mismatched chairs, and a bookcase crammed full of books on forensic science, scientific journals, and case files.

Baylor's desk was covered with stacks of paperwork, which he moved to one side. When Baylor was seated behind his desk and Charlie was seated across from him, Charlie took a stack of reports and photos from the attaché case and spread them out.

"I represent Alexis Chandler. Are you familiar with her case?"

"Just what I've seen on the news and read in the papers."

"She's got a lot of charges, but one accuses her of shooting Leon Golden."

"The defendant in the sex trafficking case?"

"Yes. She claims that she was at his estate and she shot him in self-defense, after he took a shot at her. I'd like you to take a look at the reports and photos and let me know if you can tell me if there are facts that support her claim. I can get you into the crime scene if you need to see it to draw your conclusions."

"What does Miss Chandler say happened at Golden's place?"

Charlie told Baylor what Alexis had told him. Baylor read the reports and studied the crime scene photographs.

"Interesting," Baylor said when he finished. "I will have to go to Golden's estate."

CHAPTER FORTY-NINE

IT HAD TAKEN THREE DAYS TO PICK A JURY BECAUSE OF ALL THE PUBLICITY Alexis's case had produced. When the jury was finally impaneled, Bridget and Charlie had mixed feelings about their chances.

At seven thirty the night before Charlie was going to give the opening statement in Alexis's case, he and Bridget left their office, convinced that there was nothing more they could do to prepare for the first day of *State of Oregon v. Alexis Chandler*. Neither one of them had the energy to cook, so they picked at their food at an Italian restaurant a few blocks from their condo and went home, exhausted and on edge.

When they walked into the entryway, Charlie didn't turn on the lights. Instead, he took Bridget's hand and led her into the living room so they could look out at Portland's night sky.

"Are you tired?" Charlie asked.

"I'm exhausted, but I'm too wound up to sleep."

"Do you want a glass of wine?" Charlie asked. "I've got a bottle of that good pinot we bought at that wine tasting last year."

"I had too much wine at dinner," Bridget answered as she turned to Charlie and rested her head on his shoulder. "We're going to lose this case, aren't we?" she asked.

"Maybe. I don't know. Alexis is one hell of a liar, and she's got God on her side."

"What God?"

"Read your Old Testament—the part where it talks about an eye for an eye."

"That might work if our jury was made up of twelve Barbarians. Unfortunately, Tom got rid of all the die-hard criminals and religious fanatics."

"We're doing our best, Bridget. That's all we can do. Alexis created this situation, and she's the only one who can talk her way out of it."

"Too true."

Charlie hugged Bridget. Then he kissed her. "If we got naked and fooled around, do you think you might unwind?" he asked.

Bridget laughed. "Jesus, Charlie, we have a client who might die, and all you can think about is a roll in the hay."

Charlie grinned. "I have absolutely no interest in sex. This would strictly be for medicinal purposes."

"Oh, well," Bridget said. "Making love to you usually puts me to sleep, so this might work."

"I don't turn you on?" Charlie asked, pretending that his feelings had been hurt.

"Not in the least, but you are an effective alternative to a sleeping pill, so I guess we should fool around."

WHEN CHARLIE WOKE UP, HE WAS A BUNDLE OF NERVES, HIS NORMAL state every time he was going to give an opening statement. He and Bridget forced themselves to eat a hearty breakfast packed with protein even though they had no appetite. It was going to be a long couple of weeks, and they knew from experience that they would need every ounce of energy their bodies could manufacture.

A group of reporters were waiting in the hallway outside Judge Steinbock's courtroom when Bridget and Charlie rounded the corner. They swarmed the defense team, and Charlie had to use a string of "No comment"s as a battering ram as he and his cocounsel forced their way into the packed courtroom.

Thomas Grant and Mary Choi, a deputy DA, were conferring at the prosecution counsel table when Charlie and Bridget pushed through the bar of the court.

"Good morning, Tom and Mary," Bridget said.

Grant smiled. "I expect it is going to be."

As soon as the defense team was seated, the guards led Alexis out of the holding area wearing a set of clothes that Bridget had arranged for her to wear that made her look like an attorney instead of a felon. The guards guided Alexis to a seat next to Bridget.

"What happens today?" Alexis asked.

"Charlie and the prosecutor give their opening statements," Bridget answered.

"So, are we off and running?"

"Yup," Bridget answered just as Judge Steinbock took the bench.

"Good morning, everybody," the judge said. "Are you ready to give your opening statements?"

"Ready for the State," Grant said.

"Ready for Miss Chandler," Charlie told the judge.

"Then let's bring in the jury and get started."

As soon as the jurors were seated, Thomas Grant stood and walked to the jury box.

"Good morning, ladies and gentlemen. The events that form the basis for the charges against the defendant occurred two years ago. The reason that her trial is only being held now is because she was on the run, hiding in Mexico, until she was arrested recently.

"One of the defendant's victims is a man named Leon Golden, who is serving a lengthy sentence in the Oregon State Penitentiary. Mr. Golden was a successful movie producer who lived in an estate near the Columbia River Gorge that was surrounded by a high wall decked out with razor wire and patrolled by guards with vicious dogs. Gretchen Hall, a wealthy woman who owned La Bella Roma restaurant, was Mr. Golden's coconspirator. She would lure young women, some underage, to Mr. Golden's estate with a promise that they would get a part in a motion picture. Once inside, these women became prisoners who were forced to have sex with men. One of these women was Annie Chandler, the defendant's sister. Annie was raped and murdered by Anthony Noonan, a judge on this circuit court, who is now serving a life sentence in the Oregon State Penitentiary. We know that Mr. Noonan killed Annie Chandler because we have a movie that shows the murder, which, unfortunately, you will see as part of the evidence in this case."

Grant paused to let the jurors digest this information.

"The defendant learned that Gretchen Hall had lured her sister to Golden's estate. Then her sister disappeared. Soon after, she learned that Hall and Golden had been arrested for running a sex trafficking ring.

"You will learn that the defendant is a trained sniper who served in combat in Iraq and Afghanistan. As soon as she figured out that Hall and Golden were responsible for her sister's death, she came to Oregon and went on a killing spree that left Gretchen Hall, Golden's bodyguard, Yuri Makarov, and a man named Brent Atkins dead and Mr. Golden severely wounded. She also kidnapped Detective Sally Blaisedale when she went on the run.

"Now, the defense is going to tell you about the rape and murder of Annie Chandler," Grant began the conclusion to his statement. "They are going to ask you to forgive the defendant's equally cold and calculating murders of the people involved in Leon Golden's criminal enterprise. But our society no longer permits people to take the law into their own hands. A long time ago, civilized society decided that neutral people, like yourselves, should decide if an accused should be punished, and a neutral judge should decide the punishment. That's what happened with Anthony Noonan and Leon Golden, who are serving prison sentences as punishment for the crimes they committed.

"Why do we do that? To avoid aggrieved people acting on emotion and killing innocent people, like Brent Atkins, who the defendant murdered in cold blood, even though he had no connection whatsoever to the murder of her sister.

"When all of the evidence is in, there will be no reasonable doubt in your minds that Alexis Chandler took the law into her own hands when she murdered Gretchen Hall, Yuri Makarov, and Brent Atkins, crippled Leon Golden, and kidnapped Portland detective Sally Blaisedale. Thank you."

"Mr. Webb," Judge Steinbock said.

"Thank you, Your Honor," Charlie said as he walked over to the jury box and addressed the jurors. "And thank you for taking time from your busy lives to listen to the evidence in this case.

"Now, Alexis Chandler may or may not present evidence to you. In the American judicial system created by our forefathers, a defendant in a criminal case has no duty under the Constitution to do anything.

"When the State of Oregon arrests a person, the Constitution and laws of criminal procedure require everyone to presume that the defendant is completely innocent and has done nothing wrong. Our American Constitution requires you to start this trial assuming that the State screwed up when they charged Miss Chandler, that it made a mistake.

"A district attorney starts a trial bearing the burden of proving a defendant's guilt beyond any reasonable doubt. In the American judicial system, a defendant had no burden on her to do anything. She doesn't have to produce any witnesses or evidence or cross-examine the State's witnesses. Alexis and I can go to a movie during the trial and just return for the verdict.

"Now, what do we mean when we say that the district attorney has the burden of proving Alexis is guilty beyond a reasonable doubt? This is what it means. Let's say that after hearing all of the evidence emotionally—in your heart—you feel that Miss Chandler is guilty, and unemotionally—using logic and being objective—you feel that she is guilty, but there was one single piece of evidence, like a photograph or a statement by a police officer, that raises one single reasonable doubt in your mind about her guilt; it is your patriotic duty as an American citizen to free her.

"I'm not going to tell you what the evidence will show. You'll be hearing the witnesses when I sit down. But I will ask you to refrain from drawing any conclusions about whether what Alexis did to the terrible people who callously and cruelly took her sister Annie's life constituted a crime until all of the evidence is in. Thank you."

"Call your first witness," Judge Steinbock said when Charlie was seated.

"The People call Detective Gordon Rawls."

The detective had traded his blazer and turtleneck for a banker's dark suit, white shirt, tasteful navy-blue tie, and shoes that were so well shined that they could have been mirrors. When he was seated in the witness-box, Rawls stated his name and told the jurors his professional history.

"Two years ago, were you and your partner, Detective Sally Blaisedale, tasked with the job of investigating the murder of two people whose bodies were found in Tryon Creek state park?" Grant asked.

"Yes."

"Who were the victims?"

"A Miss Gretchen Hall and a Mr. Yuri Makarov."

"Had you heard about these two people before?"

"Yes. They had been indicted, along with a Mr. Leon Golden, on charges of operating a ring that trafficked young girls for sex."

"Sometime later, did you and Detective Blaisedale go to Leon Golden's estate?"

"Yes."

"What did you find?"

"Mr. Golden had been shot in the knee and knocked unconscious."

"Did he name his assailant?"

"He said that the defendant had attacked him after blaming him for the murder of her sister."

"Did he tell you anything the defendant said about the murders of Miss Hall and Mr. Makarov?"

"Mr. Golden said that the defendant confessed to killing them."

"Was a gun found next to Mr. Golden?"

"Yes."

"Did you ask him about the gun?"

"I did."

"What did he say?"

"Objection, hearsay," Bridget said.

"May we approach?" Grant said.

Bridget, Charlie, and the prosecutor walked to the side of the judge's bench.

"Mr. Golden has been convicted of several serious crimes, and his case is being appealed," Grant said. "His lawyer won't let him testify. This is the only way we can get some very important information to the jury."

"What will Detective Rawls say Golden told him?" the judge asked.

"Golden told him that he'd never seen the gun or taken a shot at the defendant."

"Are you introducing this testimony to prove the truth of the statement?" Judge Steinbock asked.

"Yes."

"That's classic hearsay," Bridget said. "There's no way that's admissible."

"I agree," the judge said.

Grant looked frustrated. "They didn't object to some of Rawls's other testimony about what Golden said."

"We don't have to," Bridget countered, "but we are objecting to this line of questioning."

"I'm going to sustain the objection," the judge said. "Move on to another topic."

Grant composed himself so the jury wouldn't see that he'd lost, and walked back to his seat.

"Detective Rawls, was the first person you suspected of killing Miss Hall and Mr. Makarov a man named Lawrence Weiss, who also calls himself Guido Sabatini?"

"Yes."

"At some point in your investigation, did you search the woods surrounding Mr. Weiss's farm?"

"Yes."

"Did you find a dead body in the woods?"

"Yes. He was identified as Brent Atkins."

"Did the crime lab perform a ballistics test on the bullet that killed Mr. Atkins?"

"Yes."

"What did they find?"

"That bullet and the bullets that killed Miss Hall and Mr. Makarov were fired from the same gun."

"Did you receive a flash drive that contained a video of Anthony Noonan, a circuit court judge, raping and murdering a young woman named Annie Chandler?"

"Yes."

"Was Annie Chandler related to the defendant?"

"She was her sister."

The jurors looked across the courtroom at Alexis. Her head was down, and Bridget put an arm around her shoulder.

"Did you also come into possession of a voicemail that Annie Chandler sent the defendant?"

"Yes."

"Your Honor, I'd like to have the voicemail marked as State's exhibit one, and I'd like to play it for the jury."

"No objection," Charlie said.

The jurors kept watching Alexis while they listened to the voicemail. She was visibly upset.

"When you and Detective Blaisedale went to Leon Golden's estate, were you accompanied by other police officers?" Grant asked when the voicemail finished playing.

"We were. We had received information that Mr. Golden's life might be in danger."

"Did something happen to Detective Blaisedale at the estate?"

"Yes. When we arrived, the defendant ran away from Mr. Golden's house into the thick woods that bordered it. Detective Blaisedale, several officers, and I chased after her. When we couldn't find the defendant, I returned to the house and learned that Detective Blaisedale had been taken from the scene by the defendant."

"Were you able to apprehend the defendant during the days that followed the kidnapping of Detective Blaisedale?"

"No. She disappeared."

"When was she arrested?"

"Recently. We received a tip that the defendant was living in a town in Mexico. The Mexican authorities arrested her, and she waived extradition."

"Your witness," Grant said to Charlie and Bridget.

"Good morning, Detective Rawls," Bridget said.

Rawls nodded.

"Isn't it true that Miss Chandler dropped off Detective Blaisedale unharmed the next morning?"

"The defendant did let Sally out near the California-Mexico border, but she did have some injuries."

"Minor injuries?"

"Yes."

"You viewed Miss Hall's body at Tryon Creek, did you not?"

"Yes."

"Was she shot in the front?"

"Yes."

"Did you find a suitcase with fifty thousand dollars in it near her body?"

"Yes."

"And there was a handgun lying next to Miss Hall, wasn't there?"

"Yes."

"Did you view Mr. Makarov's body at the park?"

"Yes."

"Was he shot in the front?"

"Yes."

"Did he have a handgun near him?"

"Yes."

"Mr. Atkins's body was found in the woods surrounding Mr. Weiss's farm, was it not?"

"Yes."

"Did you learn that Mr. Weiss had won a lot of money from Mr. Atkins at poker?"

"Yes."

"Did you learn that Mr. Atkins and his brother had tried to rob Mr. Weiss in the parking lot of the building where the poker game was held?"

"Yes."

"You interviewed Mr. Atkins's brother, did you not?"

"Yes."

"Did he tell you that Brent Atkins had gone to Mr. Weiss's farm seeking revenge?"

"Yes."

"If you wanted to sneak up on Mr. Weiss's house, could you have gone through the woods at the point where Mr. Atkins's body was discovered?"

"Yes."

"Did Mr. Atkins have a firearm when you saw his body in the woods?"

"Yes."

"Was he shot in the front?"

"Yes."

"I don't have any more questions for Detective Rawls," Bridget said.

"The State calls Detective Sally Blaisedale."

Blaisedale cast a brief look at Alexis as she walked through the bar of the court to take the oath.

"Did you go to the estate of Leon Golden two years ago because you had received information that his life might be in danger?" Grant asked when Blaisedale was sworn.

"Yes."

"Had you been to the estate before?"

"Yes."

"Please describe the estate and the security measures Leon Golden employed when you went to the estate the first time."

The detective told the jury about the wall and the guards and dogs that patrolled the grounds.

"Tell the jury what happened at the estate when you went there on the second occasion."

Blaisedale told the jurors about being captured by Alexis during the search for her in the woods that surrounded the estate, their ride to a town near the California-Mexico border, and her subsequent release.

"Did you agree to accompany the defendant when she left Mr. Golden's estate?" Grant asked.

"No, sir. I did not."

"Did she take you from the estate to the California border by force?"

"She did."

"While you were with the defendant, did she tell you that she was the person who shot and killed Gretchen Hall and Yuri Makarov?"

"She did."

"What did she say?"

"She said, 'Those scum deserved to die for what they did to my sister and all the other girls.'"

"No further questions."

"Detective, isn't it true that you suffered almost no harm at Miss Chandler's hands?" Bridget asked.

"She put me in a choke hold, knocked me to the ground, chopped my hand, and handcuffed me."

"After Miss Chandler chopped your hand, did you have a lasting injury?"

"No."

"Did Miss Chandler choke you unconscious or just use the hold to restrain you?"

"I . . . She just held me."

"Did you have any lasting injury to your neck?"

"No."

"Did she make the handcuffs very tight?"

"No."

"Miss Chandler let you out a short distance from a small town near the California border, didn't she?"

"Yes."

"She took off the handcuffs?"

"Yes."

"Did she give you some money and tell you that there was a restaurant a mile down the road where you could get a meal?"

"Yes."

"And she told you that she would keep your phone, but she would call the local police to tell them where you were?"

"Yes."

"Did she do what she promised?"

"Yes."

"No further questions."

"No redirect," Grant said.

"It's almost noon," Judge Steinbock said. "Let's break for lunch and reconvene at one thirty."

THE REST OF THE DAY WAS TAKEN UP BY THE MEDICAL EXAMINER, WHO established the causes of death of Gretchen Hall, Yuri Makarov, and Brent Atkins; a doctor who testified about the seriousness of Leon Golden's knee injury; an army captain who testified about the military training Alexis received and the places she was deployed; and Margaret Nelson, a ballistics expert, who testified that the three murder victims were shot with the same gun.

"Mrs. Nelson, what is a GSR test?" Bridget asked when the prosecutor turned over the witness for cross-examination.

"It's a gunshot residue test. We wipe the hand of an individual to see if we can detect the distinctive chemicals that are deposited on a person's skin or clothing when a gun is fired."

"Did someone wipe Leon Golden's hand when he was found wounded at his estate?"

"Yes."

"Did you do a GSR test to see if Mr. Golden had fired a gun?"

"Yes."

"What was the result of the test?"

"It was determined that Mr. Golden had gunshot residue on his right hand."

"What about his left hand?"

"No residue was detected."

"Thank you. No further questions."

"Mr. Grant?" Judge Steinbock asked.

"The State rests, Your Honor."

"Mr. Webb, do you have some motions for the court?" the judge asked.

"We do."

"Then let's recess and take them up in the morning."

"How are we doing?" Alexis asked as Charlie started to put his papers in his briefcase.

"The defense rarely does well when the State presents its case," Charlie said as the guards approached to take Alexis back to the jail. "Our turn will come tomorrow."

CHAPTER FIFTY

IN A PRETRIAL HEARING, CHARLIE HAD TOLD THE COURT THAT THE DE-
fense wanted to show the jury the entire flash drive that contained
not only Annie's murder but the rape of several other young
women. The prosecution had asked Judge Steinbock to forbid the
playing of any part of the flash drive. Judge Steinbock had ruled
that the defense could show the jury Annie's rape and murder, but
no other part of the flash drive.

"Your Honor, I would like to show the jury defense exhibit one,
the video in which Miss Chandler's sister is raped and murdered,"
Charlie said when the jury was seated the next morning.

"I'm going to permit it, and I'm going to clear the courtroom of
any spectators who are not members of the press."

When the courtroom was cleared, Judge Steinbock turned to
the jury box. "During voir dire, the parties told you that you might
be exposed to a video that showed an actual rape and murder. All
of you said that you would be able to handle this type of graphic

violence. I've seen this video. It is not easy to watch. So, be prepared for a very disturbing experience."

No sound accompanied the video, but it was obvious that Annie Chandler was begging for her life. Alexis looked down at the counsel table while the movie ran. Charlie watched the jurors. They looked sick and upset. Two of the women and one man had tears in their eyes. All of the jurors looked at Alexis at some point during the viewing. Bridget had her arm around her client's shoulders during the viewing.

"That's over with," Bridget whispered to Alexis when the video ended.

Alexis didn't answer. Bridget handed her a glass of water. Alexis took several sips, but she didn't sit up.

"Let's take a short break," Judge Steinbock told the jurors. "And please remember that you should not discuss any of the evidence, including what you just saw, until all of the evidence is in."

"CALL YOUR FIRST WITNESS," THE JUDGE SAID WHEN THE JURORS returned.

"Miss Chandler calls Lawrence Weiss."

Charlie had convinced Guido to dress in his suit and tie, and he looked very presentable when he took the witness stand.

"Can you state your name for the record?" Charlie asked and he held his breath in hopes that his witness would use his real name as he had promised.

"My name is Lawrence Weiss."

Charlie exhaled.

"Mr. Weiss, Miss Chandler is accused of killing a man named Brent Atkins. Did you know him?"

"We had met."

"How did you meet?"

"I enjoy playing poker. There was a game that was held in the back room of a store in Clackamas County. Mr. Atkins and his brother were two of the card players at my table."

"Are you a very experienced poker player?"

"I believe I am."

"What was the result when you played against Mr. Atkins?"

Guido smiled. "Mr. Atkins was a rank beginner, and he had a tell that I identified immediately."

"Can you explain what a tell is to the jury?"

"Certainly," Guido said as he turned to the jury. "Bad poker players develop unconscious actions that give away the strength of their hands. For example, a player might scratch his nose if he is bluffing or rub his fingers together if he has a good hand. These actions are called *tells*."

"What happened when you played poker with Mr. Atkins and his brother?"

"I won a lot of their money."

"Were the brothers good losers?"

"No. When I left the game, they followed me into the parking lot with the intent of robbing me."

"Was Mr. Atkins armed?"

Guido nodded. "He had a handgun."

"Tell the jury what happened in the parking lot."

"Mr. Atkins proved to be as incompetent a robber as he was as a card player. He and his brother telegraphed their intentions, and I was able to get the drop on them before there was any violence."

"You were armed?"

"Of course. It is not unusual to run into thugs and sore losers at these games."

"Do you live in the country on a farm?"

"Yes."

"Did you install a security system on your property because of threats you received?"

"Yes."

"Did the security system detect Brent Atkins sneaking onto your property one evening with a weapon?"

"Yes."

"What did you do?"

"I left my farm and drove to the coast to avoid a confrontation."

"Thank you, Mr. Weiss. No further questions."

Thomas Grant leaned back and stared at the witness. "You gave your name as Lawrence Weiss?"

"I did."

"Do you also go by the name *Guido Sabatini*?"

"*Sì.*"

"Do you believe that you are the reincarnation of a painter who lived during the Renaissance and studied with Michelangelo and Leonardo da Vinci?"

"*Sì.*"

"Do you talk to Mr. da Vinci and Michelangelo?"

Guido laughed. "I would like to, Mr. Prosecutor, but they have been dead for centuries."

Laughter erupted in the spectator section, and even a few of the jurors chuckled, relieved to have something to laugh about after seeing the rape and murder of Annie Chandler.

"Point taken, Mr. Sabatini," Grant said in an effort to recover. "Did you study with these two gentlemen?"

"*Sì*, in another life."

"So, you actually think you spoke with Michelangelo?"

"It was before I was reborn. Perhaps you learned your excellent skills as an orator at the feet of William Jennings Bryan or Clarence Darrow in another life before your spirit entered into your mother's womb."

"Let's get back to the real world, shall we?"

"As you wish."

"You claim that you saw Mr. Atkins on your security camera."

"I did."

"Did you see a weapon in his hand?"

"Yes."

"Did you leave your farm right away, or did you arm yourself first?"

"I did secure a firearm."

"What did you plan to do?"

"I planned to get the drop on him, disarm him, and send him on his way."

"Did something happen to change your plans?"

"*Sì*, I saw another intruder closing on Mr. Atkins."

"Why didn't you stay?"

"I have since learned that Miss Chandler was this person. When I saw her in the woods, she was quite intimidating, all dressed in black with a ski mask, like a ninja, and armed as well." Guido shrugged. "You know what they say about discretion being the better part of valor. I decided it was time to go."

"So, you saw the defendant sneaking up on Brent Atkins in the dark in the woods with a gun?"

"Yes."

"No further questions."

"I don't have any," Charlie said. "May Mr. Weiss be excused?"

"Yes. Who is your next witness?"

"Miss Chandler calls Paul Baylor.

"Mr. Baylor, did I ask you to examine the alleged crime scene in Leon Golden's mansion?" Charlie asked as soon as the forensic expert told the jurors his academic and professional credentials.

"Yes."

"Why did I ask you to do that?"

"Your client claimed that Mr. Golden had fired a gun at her. You wanted to know if the evidence at the scene would support her assertion."

"What did you conclude?"

"I concluded that the evidence was consistent with her assertion."

"Why did you reach that conclusion?"

"I observed a bullet hole in the wall next to the front door. A police report confirmed that a bullet had been extracted from the hole, and a ballistics expert at the Oregon State Crime Lab reported that the bullet had been fired from a weapon that was found next to Mr. Golden.

"I learned Mr. Golden's height and the distance from the floor to his right shoulder. Mr. Golden is right-handed, and the handgun that was discovered at the scene was near his right hand. I also learned that a test had established the presence of a significant amount of gunshot residue—hundreds of characteristic particles—on Mr. Golden's right hand and no particles on his left hand. So, I assumed that he would have fired the weapon with his right hand.

"Next, I fixed the trajectory that the bullet would have followed if Mr. Golden fired the gun while standing. I concluded that the bullet from Mr. Golden's gun would have ended up in the vicinity where the bullet was found if he was aiming at someone standing in the front door and missed his mark."

"Your witness, Mr. Grant."

"Thank you, Mr. Webb. Mr. Baylor, you said that you concluded that the scenario at the crime scene was consistent with the defendant's claim that Mr. Golden had fired a gun at her?"

"Yes."

"Let's assume that the defendant knocked Mr. Golden unconscious and determined where his right shoulder would be if he was standing. Then assume that she raised Mr. Golden to his feet, fitted the gun in his hand, used Mr. Golden's finger to fire the gun from the appropriate height, and left the gun next to Mr. Golden's unconscious body. Would you also say that the scene was consistent with this scenario?"

Baylor thought before answering, "I guess that scenario is possible, but unlikely."

"But it is possible?" Grant asked.

Baylor shrugged. "Anything is possible."

"No further questions."

"Mr. Webb?" the judge asked.

"Nothing further. May the witness be excused?"

"You may step down, Mr. Baylor. Any more witnesses, Mr. Webb?"

Charlie leaned over to his client. "You're on, Alexis. Bridget is going to handle the direct examination. Remember what we told you. Talk to the jurors as if they were friends who were at your house for dinner and wanted to know about your case. The people in the jury box are just ordinary people, and they want to hear what you have to say.

"When Grant cross-examines, don't be combative, answer honestly, don't be afraid to say you don't know an answer or aren't sure, if that's the truth."

"Okay," Alexis said.

Bridget stood. "The defense calls Alexis Chandler."

A murmur passed through the spectator section, and the jurors sat up and focused on the witness-box as Alexis took her seat.

"Please tell the jury your name," Bridget said after Alexis was sworn.

Alexis turned to the jury box. "My name is Alexis Elin Chandler."

"Where were you born?"

"Scranton, Pennsylvania."

"Are your parents still alive?"

"No, they were both killed in a car crash."

"Who remained in your family after your parents passed?"

"Just me and my sister, Annie."

"Were you close?"

"Very close. We did a lot together when we were in the same town and talked a lot during the week when we lived in different places."

"Did you go to high school in Scranton?"

"Yes."

"Did you do well academically?"

"I graduated fourth in my class."

"Were you involved in track?"

"Yes."

"How did you do?"

"I was third in the state in cross-country, and I won the mile at the state championships in my senior year after placing in my sophomore and junior years."

"Did your athletic and academic accomplishments earn you a scholarship to UCLA?"

"Yes."

"Did something happen in your sophomore year that derailed your college career?"

"Yes."

"Tell the jury what happened."

"The team won the Pac-12 track championship, and I was in a tavern near the campus celebrating with my teammates. Some members of the football team were there, and they were drunk and obnoxious. One of them put his arm around me and tried to kiss me. I told him to stop, and so did the other women, but he would go away and come back.

"The last time, he grabbed my breast and squeezed so hard it hurt. I was holding a beer mug, and I was very angry. I smashed it in his face, and a piece of glass lodged in his eye. When he reeled back, I continued to attack him, and I injured him severely enough so he had to go to the hospital.

"The police arrested me, even though everyone said I was acting in self-defense. The player I injured was from a rich family, and they put a lot of pressure on the DA. My father served with distinction in the military. To make a long story short, I made a plea deal where the charges would be dropped if I went into the army."

"Where did you serve?"

"I did tours in Iraq and Afghanistan."

"In combat?"

"I was a sniper."

"Can you tell the jurors about some of the action you saw?"

"I can't, Miss Fournier. Most of what I did is classified. The army won't let me talk about it."

"It was in service to your country, the United States of America?"

"Yes."

"Did you receive commendations and medals for the things you did?" Bridget asked.

"Yes."

"Did you receive training on computers and other areas of technology?"

"Yes."

"Specifically, did you learn how to place wiretaps and other surveillance technology in a building?"

"Yes."

"Did you leave the army?"

"Yes."

"What did you do after you left?"

"I went back to UCLA to finish my degree."

"At some point, did you leave California and move to Oregon?"

"Yes."

"Why did you do that?"

Alexis looked down and took a deep breath. When she looked back at the jury, she had still not regained her composure. "It was Annie."

"What about her?"

"She was living in Portland, and I got this excited voicemail from her."

"Is this the voicemail that the jury heard in which she told you that she'd met Gretchen Hall, who was taking her to the estate of Leon Golden to audition for a part in a film?"

"Yes."

"I'd like to play the voicemail again," Bridget said.

"No objection," Thomas Grant said.

The bailiff played the voicemail.

"Was that the last time you heard from Annie?" Bridget asked.

"Yes."

"What did you do?"

"I called her, but the messages went to voicemail. I didn't know any of her friends."

"Has Annie's body been recovered?"

"No. I didn't know what happened to her. Then I heard that Leon Golden and a woman named Gretchen Hall had been arrested for sex trafficking young women, and I flew to Portland."

"When you came to Portland, did you use the name *Elin Crane?*"

"Yes."

"Why did you do that?"

"I wanted to find the people responsible for murdering Annie, and I didn't want anyone making the connection if I used the name *Chandler.*"

"What did you do when you got there?"

"I found out where Leon Golden lived, and I broke into his house and installed listening devices."

"Did you hear anything that helped you find out what had happened to Annie?"

"I learned that Golden, Gretchen Hall, and others were panicking because an artist named Guido Sabatini, whose real name is Lawrence Weiss, had taken a flash drive from a safe in Hall's restaurant that contained crucial evidence that the DA could use to convict the people who were charged in the sex trafficking case and Annie's murder."

"Did they specifically mention your sister?"

"They never used her last name, but once, when talking about the murder, they used her first name. I also learned that Mr. Sabatini was willing to return the flash drive to Hall if she would hang a painting he'd sold her in the dining room of her restaurant. If that happened, the evidence would be lost."

"What did you do next?"

"I decided to steal the flash drive from Mr. Sabatini. I put on dark clothing and went through the woods that surrounded his farm."

"Did you encounter someone in the woods?"

"Yes. There was a man in front of me. I learned later that he was Brent Atkins. I assumed he was going to harm Mr. Sabatini because he was sneaking up on the farm."

"What happened next?"

"I came up behind him."

"What were you planning to do?"

"I wanted to protect Mr. Sabatini. If something happened to him, the flash drive might be lost."

"Were you planning to kill Mr. Atkins?"

"No. I wanted to disable him so he couldn't hurt Mr. Sabatini. Then I was hoping to persuade Mr. Sabatini to give me the flash drive so I could give it to the police."

"What happened?"

"Mr. Atkins heard me and turned. He had a gun, and I shot him."

"Why did you do that?"

"I thought he would shoot me."

"So, you shot him in self-defense to save your own life?"

"Yes."

"What did you do next?"

"I hurried to the farm to see if I could convince Mr. Sabatini to give me the flash drive, but he'd left. I learned later that he had a security system and had seen me and Mr. Atkins on his equipment."

"Did you do anything else to find out what had happened to Annie?" Bridget asked.

"I called Gretchen Hall and told her that I had the flash drive and would sell it to her for fifty thousand dollars. I arranged to meet her at night in Tryon Creek state park."

"Why did you do that?"

"I planned to force her to tell me what happened to Annie."

"What happened in the park?"

"I found a place to lie up in the park way ahead of the meet so I could see if Hall would try and double-cross me."

"You used the skills you'd developed as a sniper?"

"Yes."

"Did Hall do something that alarmed you?"

"She sent Yuri Makarov to ambush me."

"What did you do?"

"When I saw Hall walk into the park, I confronted Makarov. He tried to shoot me, but I was faster and shot him."

"So, you shot Mr. Makarov in self-defense to save your own life?"

"Yes."

"What happened next?"

"Miss Hall must have heard me, because she tried to shoot me."

"How did you react?"

"I shot her in self-defense."

"To save your own life?"

"Yes."

"Did she bring fifty thousand dollars to the meet?"

"Yes, but I had no interest in her money. I just wanted to find out what happened to Annie, so I left the money."

"At some point, did you learn what happened to Annie?"

"Yes. Mr. Sabatini agreed to turn over the flash drive to me and Judge Anthony Noonan. We were alone in Mr. Sabatini's barn. Mr. Sabatini had seen what was on the drive, and he knew what the judge had done to my sister." Alexis stopped.

"Do you want some water?" Bridget asked.

Alexis nodded.

"Would you like to take a break?" Judge Steinbock asked.

"No. I want to get this over with," Alexis said in a voice that was barely audible.

"Do you feel you can tell the jury what happened in the barn?" Bridget asked when Alexis drank from a glass of water.

"Yes. Mr. Sabatini said that the video showed Judge Noonan raping and killing Annie. Noonan pulled out a gun, and Mr. Sabatini . . . he stabbed him in the eye with a paintbrush. He saved my life."

"So, you learned that Annie had been murdered by Anthony Noonan, and Leon Golden was responsible for her being held as a sex slave?"

"Yes."

"What did you do?"

"I went to Golden's estate to force him to confess."

"Not to kill him?"

"No. I wanted him to suffer in prison, and I needed him to tell the police the names of the other men who had abused the young women he held prisoner at his estate."

"What happened at Golden's mansion?"

"When I went into his house, he tried to shoot me, but he missed. I didn't want to kill him, so I shot him in the knee."

"What happened then?"

"I forced him to give a taped confession that I sent to the police."

"What happened next?"

"The police arrived, and I ran out a side door into the woods. Detective Blaisedale followed me, and I disarmed her and used her to get a car so I could escape."

"Alexis, you're charged with the murder of Gretchen Hall and Yuri Makarov. Did you plan on killing them?"

"No. I'm not sad that they're dead. They were horrible, evil people who . . . They were responsible for killing my Annie. But I shot them in self-defense."

"What about Brent Atkins?"

"I feel terrible about that. He had nothing to do with Annie's murder. But I was trying to protect Mr. Sabatini, and I defended myself when he tried to shoot me."

"What about the charge that you assaulted Mr. Golden?"

"He tried to kill me when I walked in his front door. I was lucky he missed and I didn't shoot to kill. I just wanted to disable him so he couldn't shoot at me anymore. I needed him alive to get him to confess to the horrible things he'd done."

"Thank you, Alexis. We have no further questions," Bridget said.

"I think this would be a good time to take a break," Judge Steinbock said.

"You were great," Charlie said when Alexis was seated beside him and the jury and judge had left the courtroom.

"I don't feel great. That was very hard."

"It might get harder. Grant questions you next."

Alexis looked at Charlie. "I told the truth, Charlie. Don't they say the truth will set you free?"

The guards took Alexis away so she could use the restroom.

"What do you think?" Charlie asked Bridget.

"I don't believe a word she said about shooting Hall, Makarov, Golden, and Atkins, but I was watching the jurors, and I think she created a lot of sympathy and, just maybe, a reasonable doubt."

"I'M SORRY THAT YOU LOST YOUR SISTER UNDER SUCH HORRIBLE CIRcumstances," Thomas Grant told Alexis at the start of his cross-examination.

"Thank you."

"Do you agree that losing a loved one under those circumstances can make a person do things they normally wouldn't do?"

"Yes."

"You seem like a well-educated woman. Can I assume you know that it is against the law for anyone, no matter how badly they have suffered at the hands of a criminal, to take the law into their own hands?"

"Yes."

"You know by now that my office has sent the man who killed Annie to prison for life and that Mr. Golden is also in the Oregon State Penitentiary along with other people who participated in Mr. Golden's sex ring."

"Yes."

"Do you understand that the people of Oregon did that by using the courts and our criminal justice system, and not by resorting to vigilante justice?"

"Yes."

"Miss Chandler, do you think of yourself as someone who is basically honest?"

"Yes."

"When you arrived in Portland, were you honest when you told people your name?"

"I used a false name to disguise my connection to Annie."

"You did more than that. Didn't you insinuate yourself into Charles Webb's law practice by pretending to be someone named Elin Crane?"

"Mr. Webb was representing Guido Sabatini, and I wanted to get close to him so I could convince him to give me or the authorities the flash drive."

"Can I assume that someone with your military background has elite skills with weapons?"

"I don't understand the question."

"Are you an expert markswoman?"

"Yes."

"Skilled enough to disable Leon Golden when you had a choice to shoot him in the knee instead of killing him?"

"I did that."

"From your testimony, I take it that you wanted Gretchen Hall to tell you what happened to your sister."

"Yes."

"Could someone with your level of skill have disabled Miss Hall, the way you disabled Mr. Golden, instead of killing her?"

"That was not an option in the park. It was dark, she had her gun pointed at me, and I didn't have time to think."

"You testified that you confronted Mr. Makarov."

"Yes."

"So, you had the drop on him. You surprised him."

"Yes."

"But you chose to kill him and not incapacitate him."

"When I told him to lower his weapon, he brought it up very fast. I had no choice."

"Did the army train you in hand-to-hand combat?"

"Yes."

"Are you skilled in that area?"

"I am."

"Are you telling this jury that, with all your highly skilled combat training, you couldn't take Brent Atkins from behind?"

"I was planning to, but he heard me and turned with his gun pointed at me before I could get close enough."

"Let's talk about Guido Sabatini, Miss Chandler. You told the jury that you wanted to get close to him so you could convince him to turn over the flash drive to you or the authorities."

"Yes."

"Didn't you take some drastic steps to obtain this result?"

"I don't understand the question."

"Didn't you frame Mr. Sabatini for Gretchen Hall's murder by draping one of his paintings over her body and planting the gun you used to shoot her in his farmhouse?"

"Yes. I believed that he would turn over the drive if he was arrested for murder."

"There was another possibility, wasn't there?"

"I don't understand your question."

"Wasn't Mr. Sabatini tried for a murder that you committed?"

"It wasn't murder. I acted in self-defense."

"That's what you claim, but you made it look as if Mr. Sabatini had murdered Miss Hall in cold blood, a crime that could have sent an innocent person to death row."

"I never intended that to happen."

"But it almost did, because you were willing to do anything, without regard for the law, to avenge your sister. I have no further questions."

CHAPTER FIFTY-ONE

BY THE TIME CHARLIE AND BRIDGET WALKED BACK TO THEIR OFFICE, Alexis was back in the jail and there were no reporters around, so Charlie didn't have to put on a happy face.

"Fucking Grant," Charlie swore.

"His cross was very good," Bridget said.

"Do you think it was good enough to tip the jury in his favor?"

"I don't know."

"Any ideas?" Charlie asked.

"I do have one. I've been watching the jurors. I think a lot of them understand how much Alexis has suffered, and they've got to be horrified after seeing the snuff film. I thought Alexis made a pretty good self-defense argument that could create a reasonable doubt in the murder and assault charges, and she may have gotten enough sympathy to give us a hung jury, even if the jury doesn't acquit on the crimes of violence. But Grant has Alexis cold on the kidnapping."

"You want to propose a plea deal," Charlie said.

Bridget nodded.

"Let's call Tom."

THOMAS GRANT WAS SITTING BEHIND HIS DESK. HE DID NOT LOOK happy when Bridget and Charlie walked into his office, and he did not stand up. Mary Choi was sitting on a sofa that was against the wall and across from her boss. Charlie smiled at her, but she didn't return the smile and showed no expression.

"On the phone, you said that you wanted to discuss a deal," Grant said as the defense team sat opposite him on the other side of his desk.

"Alexis Chandler is a patriot, a decorated soldier," Charlie started.

"I respect that, but serving your country doesn't give you a free pass if you murder someone."

"Agreed, but Alexis told the jury that she acted in self-defense."

Grant smirked. "And you believe her?"

"What I believe doesn't matter," Charlie said. "It's what the jury believes. Did you get a good look at the jurors when we played the film that showed Annie Chandler being raped and murdered? Did you see their reactions while Alexis was testifying? Several of the jurors were crying."

"That gut reaction to a horrifying experience may change when they have time to calm down and think about the evidence."

"And it may not. I'd say that, right now, you have jurors that want to believe Alexis, and that adds up to an acquittal or a hung jury."

"What do you propose, Charlie?"

"We think Alexis is going to get a lot of sympathy from the jurors on the homicides and the wounding of Golden. We also think that her self-defense explanation for what happened raises a substantial reasonable doubt. But there's the kidnapping count. You have a strong case. Let Alexis plead to that charge, and drop the rest. Then decide on a reasonable sentence. What do you say?"

"Let me think about it, and let's talk in the morning."

THE NEXT MORNING, JUDGE STEINBOCK TOLD THE GUARDS TO LET ALEXIS and her lawyers meet in the jury room in the courtroom next to his.

"What's up?" Alexis asked when she saw how serious her attorneys looked.

"We have a way to end your trial, but we need you to agree with what we propose."

"Okay."

"We met with Grant after court yesterday. He recognizes that your self-defense claims and the sympathy you're getting from the jury could end up with acquittals or a hung jury in the charges involving Golden, Hall, Makarov, and Atkins. But we all agree that he has you cold on the kidnapping charge.

"Grant is willing to entertain a plea to the kidnapping charge. If you agree, he'll dismiss the other charges."

"How much time will I have to do?"

"Five years. With good behavior, you could be out in a lot less."

"I don't really have a choice, do I?"

"It's a really great offer," Bridget said.

Alexis was quiet for a few minutes, and her lawyers let her think.

"Okay," she said. "Let's get this over with."

CHAPTER FIFTY-TWO

CHARLIE AND ALEXIS WERE SITTING IN THE JURY ROOM. THE JUDGE HAD dismissed the jurors and taken the plea. In chambers, he'd told the parties that he was glad that the case had been resolved the way it had, and he wished Alexis good luck. When the hearing was over, Charlie told Bridget that he wanted to have a few moments alone with their client.

"It's just the two of us, and the attorney-client privilege is still in effect."

Alexis smiled. "What do you want to know, Charlie?"

"Did you ambush Makarov, and did you ambush Gretchen Hall and plant Hall's gun at the park?"

"What do you think?"

"I am sure you did, because I am certain that you planned on killing Gretchen Hall before you lured her into the park."

"Are you a mind reader?"

"No, Alexis, you made a fatal mistake. Fortunately for you, Tom Grant never picked up on it."

"Enlighten me."

"You planted the weapon you used to murder Hall in Guido's house *after* you killed her, but you took Guido's painting *before* you lured Hall into the park. If you weren't planning on killing Gretchen Hall, why would you bring Guido's painting to the park? If she were alive, she would be able to tell the police that Mr. Sabatini wasn't her attacker. The only answer is that you planned on killing Hall all along."

"You're a lot smarter than people think you are, Charlie."

"I don't know if that's a compliment or not."

"It is definitely a compliment."

"There are a few more things I'd like cleared up."

"Like what?"

"Like what really happened at Leon Golden's estate."

"What do you think happened?"

Charlie looked Alexis in the eye. "I think Thomas Grant's unlikely scenario happened. Golden said that he never had a gun and that he never tried to shoot you. He says that you shot him in the kneecap and forced him to confess while you recorded the confession. Then he said that you knocked him out and planted the gun they found next to him.

"You know a lot about firearms, and snipers have to know angles, so figuring out how to make it look like Golden fired at a specific spot shouldn't have been hard for you. And you're pretty strong. I imagine you could have lifted up Golden, even if he was unconscious, then fitted that gun in his hand and manipulated his finger to take the shot that was found in the door."

Alexis smiled. "Is there anything else you'd like to know?"

"So, no comment."

"Exactly."

"Okay, one more question. Atkins. Was that really self-defense?" Charlie asked.

Alexis stopped smiling. "That's the only thing I've done that I regret, but I really had no choice. It was like I said. It was pitch black, he heard me and turned with the gun up. I didn't have time to think.

"And now I have a question of my own, Charlie. If I did kill Makarov and Hall in cold blood and I did plant the gun they found next to Golden, would you regret getting me this deal?"

"Not in the least. If there'd been some way that I could have arranged for you to walk out of court a free woman, I would have done it without a single regret."

"Even with the way I used you?"

"I've always been a sucker for a pretty face."

"Are things good with you and Bridget?"

"They couldn't be better."

"I'm happy for you, Charlie, and I'm very happy about the way you've evolved from the insecure person you were when I met you."

"You had something to do with that."

"I'd like to think I did."

Charlie stood up. "I'm going to keep in touch. If you need me at your parole hearing, let me know. I'll be there, free of charge."

"Thanks. Can I consider you a friend?"

"Always."

GARY AND BOB HAD BEEN IN COURT EVERY DAY OF ALEXIS'S TRIAL, AND they were waiting in the corridor outside the courtroom for Bridget and Charlie.

"You're fucking magicians," Gary said.

"That's not what he was saying before you got that insane plea deal," Bob said. "He bet me a hundred bucks that Chandler was going down on the murder charges."

"Thanks for believing in me, asshole," Charlie told Gary.

"I lost my bet, but I'm really glad Alexis won't be in the pokey for very long," Gary said. "I think she's hot. Do you think you can put in a word for me when she gets out?"

"Definitely," Bridget said. "The word I'll say is 'RUN!'"

Gary and Bob laughed.

"We got to celebrate," Bob said. "Let's head to the Buccaneer. Drinks and eats on us."

"We're pretty beat, guys," Bridget said. "Can we get a rain check?"

"You bet," Bob said.

WHEN THEY WERE WALKING BACK TO THEIR OFFICE, CHARLIE TOLD BRID-get about his conversation with Alexis.

"How are you feeling?" Bridget asked.

"Good."

"She lied under oath in court, and she lied to you from the get-go."

"True, but I don't regret the outcome. I feel sick every time I remember what we saw on that film. If someone had done that to you, I don't know what I would have done. And don't forget what those monsters did to all those other girls."

"I know you have reservations about what Alexis did, but I feel really good about the way this case ended. Sometimes a person does something that's against the law that you can't help feeling is justified. That's what this case was always about."

Bridget leaned over and planted a kiss on Charlie's cheek. "You're a good man," she said.

"I'm glad you think so, because you're stuck with me."

ACKNOWLEDGMENTS

THE BOOK YOU READ IS DIFFERENT FROM THE FIRST DRAFT I WRITE. THE final product is the result of the thoughtful comments of my editor, Keith Kahla, one of the best in the business; copyedits; the cover developed by the art department; and the work of many other members of the team at Minotaur. So, thank you Rob Grom, Grace Gay, Martin Quinn, Hector DeJean, Paul Hochman, Omar Chapa, Alisa Trager, Kenneth J. Silver, David Rotstein, Chris Ensey and Sara Robb, Katy Robitzski, and Tracy Roe for your hard work. It is appreciated.

I am very lucky to be represented by my brilliant agent, Jennifer Weltz, who has made it possible for me to enjoy a fabulous career doing something I love. Thanks too for the great help I get from other members of the Jean V. Naggar Literary Agency, Alice Tasman, Ariana Philips, and Cole Hildebrand.

Finally, I want to thank my wonderful wife, Melanie Nelson, for making my life away from writing an adventure.

ABOUT THE AUTHOR

Anthony Georgis

Phillip Margolin is the author of over twenty-five novels, many of them *New York Times* bestsellers, including *Gone, But Not Forgotten* and *The Third Victim*. A prominent criminal defense attorney for many years, he lives in Portland, Oregon.